THE DOCTOR'S NANNY

Tennessee Tulanes

IVY JAMES

Kindred Spirits Publishing

*This book has a clean and wholesome version by Kay Lyons titled THE NANNY'S SECRET. Ivy James is the alter-ego of Kay Lyons, who now focuses on sweet/clean and wholesome contemporary romance and romantic suspense. For more information about Ivy's slightly sexier novels (or to find Kay's clean and wholesome versions of them as well as her latest titles), please go to Ivy James Author/Kay Lyons Author. Or, find her at one of the following:

@KayLyonsAuthor (Twitter)

Kay Lyons Author (Facebook)

Author_Kay_Lyons (Instagram)

Kay Lyons, Author (Pinterest)

Chapter 1

SHE SHOULD HAVE REALIZED her perfect little sister would one day grow up to be the perfect little newly wedded wife, with the perfect house in the country, the perfect brand-new car in the driveway. It was all so…

"Perfect," she whispered to herself. Megan Rose curled her fingers around the steering wheel, the split leather duct-taped together and sticky beneath her palms.

Growing up, she and Jenn had rarely seen eye to eye on things, mostly because Jenn was a thinker and Megan was a doer and doers generally acted first and thought things through later, thereby regularly ticking the thinkers off.

Megan sagged in the seat and went over the speech in her head, the one she'd spent the past eight hours practicing, when all she longed to do was leave. And why not? Hell hadn't frozen over and yet here she was in Beauty, Tennessee, begging her goody-two-shoes little sister for help. This would never work.

Unbidden, she glanced beside her at a portion of the accumulated remainder of her life. Packed in a small, single suitcase and duffel, her clothes were piled in the passenger seat, the trunk full of boxes. Behind her, a pillow and blanket were tossed haphazardly aside.

Unbuckling her seat belt, she stretched to reach the pillow and blanket and shoved them into the leg space behind her seat. There. Everyone traveling long distances had a pillow in the car, didn't they? She coughed weakly, dread colliding with fear and a boatload of you-should've-known-betters along the way.

Jenn's gonna slam that glossy black door in your face.

If so, then Megan would deal with it. She owed Jenn an apology and, once that was done, if Jenn still didn't forgive her, well, whatever. Megan would move on to Plan B.

Plan B being?

She stared at the entry, at the pumpkins lining the steps, the scarecrow winking at her with its freaky little face. Witch, jack-o'-lantern and ghost window clings filled the windows around the door, but the old-fashioned wrought-iron light fixtures flanking each side of the structure gave it the Jenn-like cuteness that grated on Megan's last nerve. Couldn't her baby sister have one flaw? Did everything have to be so Martha-Freaking-Stewart perfect all the time?

The only ugly thing on the property presently was her nightmare on wheels. She should've parked down the street and walked to the house. But it wasn't too late. Jenn didn't know Megan was outside. She'd been sitting here a couple minutes staring at the electric candles in the windows and the door bedecked with a glorious fall wreath, and no one inside the two-story home was aware of her presence cluttering up the pristine driveway. And since Jenn hadn't seen her…

Scrambling, Megan turned the key to make her getaway and swore when the car coughed, sputtered and rattled like a chain-smoker but didn't start. *Come on, leave me an ounce of pride.*

Nothing.

Megan lowered her forehead to the steering wheel. She'd coasted into town on fumes, and $3.23 wasn't going to get much in the way of gas, food or shelter. She needed a place to stay and, like it or not, Jenn's *was* the last place on earth. The last place Megan wanted to be, the last place she was welcome.

The last place Sean will look for you. He won't come here. He'd never come here, not when he knows how Jenn feels about you.

A self-deprecating smile pulled at her lips. The saying was true—paybacks were hell. Pride was a sin and this was her punishment. "You're eatin' crow, Megs. Better grab the salt."

Inhaling and coughing as a result, she ignored the tightness in her chest and the fatigue that made her want to curl up in a ball and pushed upright, climbing out of the car before she could wimp out. *Just play it easy. You're here for a visit, here to apologize. That's not a lie. Jenn doesn't have to know all the nasty details.*

She winced at the blinding sun shining down from the cloud-spotted sky. The late-September day was bright and beautiful, a balmy seventy-four degrees. But she didn't feel the warmth. Another cough racked her as she straightened her shoulders, smoothed her features and attempted to psych herself up for the confrontation to come.

"Je veux partir! Je veux aller à la maison!"

Megan blinked at the rapid-fire French. That wasn't something often heard in Small Town, U.S.A. She couldn't tell if it was coming from Jenn's or a neighbor's, but the high, shrill voice of the kid indicated he wanted to leave and he wanted to do it now.

Join the club, kid.

"Simon, no. Simon!"

Dave's shout from *Alvin and the Chipmunks* sounded in her head. Wrong character since Alvin was the one always getting yelled at, but the memory was there all the same. If anything, she was Alvin and Jenn—Jenn was Simon, a brainiac always showing off how smart he was and saying "I told you so."

She's going to say it. You know she's going to.

Megan ignored the harping voice in her head and marched her aching body up the walk to the steps, fighting the urge to kick one of the pumpkins off its perch. Distracted, she tripped and nearly fell, her grip on the iron railing the only thing that kept her from making an even bigger fool of herself than showing up on Jenn's doorstep like the beggar she now was.

How could a matter of days change so many things? Since leaving Sean she'd lived pretty much paycheck to paycheck, but after leaving California…

You didn't have to take off last time. That guy asking about you was probably just a coincidence.

Maybe. But her instincts screamed that there were no coincidences and she wasn't willing to take the risk.

By the time Megan reached the door, her legs trembled. What would Jenn do? Say? Would she invite her in or tell her to F-off?

Biting her lip, Megan forced her hand up and knocked twice. Just breathe, say you're sorry, and see what happens. Besides, sweet Jenn doesn't use that kind of language. If anything, she'll be polite when she tells you to get lost.

Her pulse pounded in her ears, and she gripped the railing in her fist. She stood here on this stupid landing like a door-to-door salesman. *No choice, remember?*

Megan eyed the new Honda parked in front of the garage. It had to be Jenn's. The last time she'd talked to her father he'd told her that Jenn's husband was the tall, dark and brooding type. No way would a guy like that drive the cute little Civic. A pearly white, it had a pair of miniature flip-flops dangling from the rearview mirror and screamed *happy bride*.

So don't screw it up for her. Leave her alone. Take one of the sleazeball sex offers if you have to. What do you have to lose? Respect? Dignity? You lost those when you crawled through the mud at Sean's feet.

"*Je veux partir! Je veux aller à la maison!*"

Now that definitely sounded as if it came from the back of the house.

Megan carefully retraced her steps, defiantly nudging a pumpkin off its post on the way down and pretending she didn't notice it fall into the mulch with a dull *thump*. Back at her Buick, she fought the urge to climb in and take off, and then remembered she couldn't go anywhere because the ugly thing wouldn't start. Didn't that just suck.

Megan walked alongside the garage to the back of the house and, sure enough, there was Jenn. Her sister stood beneath a tree staring up at leaves hinting at a cheerful shade of orange-red.

Jenn looked exactly the same. She still had that beautiful, Marilyn Monroe hourglass shape with full breasts and curvy hips, whereas Megan had learned Victoria's true secret before she'd hit puberty.

That's why scarecrows freak you out. You look like them.

Megan waited for Jenn to notice her, but Jenn's attention was focused entirely up in the tree. What was she looking at? Megan squinted and finally spotted severely thin, short black legs dangling above Jenn's head, just out of reach.

"Simon, sweetheart, I'm sorry. I don't understand you. I know you want Ethan, but he had to go to the hospital.

You know, the *hospital?* He'll be back soon. Now, please, come down."

"Je veux aller à la maison."

"Simon, come down. You're going to get hurt." Jenn pointed to the ground and waited expectantly.

Perfect, patient Jenn. The kid looked comfortable enough in the tree. Simon's blindingly white, black-and-red Nike Shox were paired with equally clean khaki-colored shorts and a bright green T-shirt with an emblem over the pocket. The clothes hung on the boy, not fitting his too-thin frame and birdlike legs.

Megan moved closer and got a look at the kid's face. Poor thing. His cheeks were streaked with tears and the boy shook nearly as much as she did at facing Jenn, which was funny considering Jenn was about as scary as Thumper.

So why are you so freaked out?

Because Jenn was Jenn, perfect in every way. Megan would bet her baby sis had never had to sleep in her car or forgo meals because of life's little backhanded jokes.

"Je ne veux pas rester ici. Je veux Dr. Ethan!"

"Simon—"

"He wants to go home, to Dr. Ethan."

Jenn whirled around so fast she stumbled before she caught herself by placing a hand against the trunk of the tree. The breeze picked up and the fallen leaves rustled around them, the clouds overhead moving to cover the sun in a perfectly timed moment so highly dramatic any director would've been moved to tears and screaming for his Oscar.

To Megan, it just confirmed what she'd learned years ago. God had a quirky sense of humor. And given her behavior of times past, she'd learned she was usually on the receiving end of it.

Just trying to change your ways, Megan. You can't fault Him for that. How many times had her mother said that to her in her oh-so-prim voice?

Megan watched as Jenn's expression changed from startled and flushed to one of utter disbelief. Jenn's mouth flattened into a tight ridge, her face turning as pale as the sheets fluttering behind her on the clothesline.

"You've got to be kidding me."

O-kay. Megan dug deep and managed a smile. "Trick or treat."

Chapter 2

JENN BLINKED AT HER a couple times in obvious disbelief. "What are you doing here? And what on earth happened to your hair?"

Megan smoothed a hand over her recently dyed brown locks. She hoped the change in hair color might buy her some time since Sean and his investigators—should her suspicions be correct—would be looking for a blond. She took a tentative step closer. "I came to see you," she said, lifting her hand toward her hair. "And I felt the need for a change."

She couldn't hold Jenn's gaze for long so she locked sights with the kid up in the tree. Cute. Young, maybe five or six years old, and definitely too thin, but cute. He watched them with interest, his sniffling cries momentarily halted in the face of the distraction and the drama playing out before him.

The kid was upset but not overly so. Just making a fuss. He looked more tired than anything, his long, thick lashes falling low over the most gorgeous caramel-honey-colored eyes she'd ever seen. What a heartbreaker. *"Elle a peur que tu te fasses mal, Simon. S'il te plaît, descends delà."*

"What did you tell him?"

Jenn could be *so* suspicious. Then again, how many times had Megan given her baby sis reason to be? "I told him you were going to make him eat worms if he didn't mind you."

Jenn gasped. "Megan!"

Megan rubbed her pounding head. "I'm kidding. I said you're afraid he'll get hurt, and that he should come down."

"Je veux aller chez moi. Je ne l'aime pas ici."

"He wants to go home. He doesn't like it here."

"Home! Home!"

Jenn turned back to the boy. She held up her arms and coaxed him with a come-here waggle of her fingers. "I know you want to go home, honey. And you will. *Soon.* Come down. Please?"

The kid stubbornly shook his head and Jenn dropped her arms with a put-out sigh. Megan had a hard time hiding a smirk. She liked this kid. Trying not to cough, she asked, "Want me to try?"

"Fine. See what you can do. But just remember he's five, not twenty-five."

Megan widened her eyes and ignored the stabs of pain shooting through her head as a result. Jeez, her head hurt, her chest had an elephant sitting on it and Jenn worried about her doing something to the kid? "What, no sex jokes or come-ons?"

"Megan."

Megan wrapped her arms over her front in an attempt to keep warm. The sun had peeked back out from behind the clouds, but wasn't heating her up.

"Just get him down in one piece. I'm responsible for Simon and don't want anything to happen to him."

"He's in a tree. What would I do to him?"

Jenn harrumphed. "Anything's possible with you. We both know good and well that boundaries or restrictions aren't your thing."

And there it was. Strike number one. That didn't take long, now did it?

Megan bit her tongue, glad the breeze blew her hair in her face and allowed her to pretend Jenn's comment hadn't struck home. Sleeping in your car had a way of humbling a girl. After all, it was kind of hard to put others in their place when you'd been put into yours.

If that's all she says to you, you need to buy a lottery ticket.

Megan shifted her feet, her legs aching like she'd run a marathon. "Why don't you go get something to help entice him down." She nodded toward Jenn's comfy-looking house and wished she could go inside to warm up. "Candy or something?"

Jenn hesitated and Megan could practically see Jenn's mind running wild with all the potential scenarios, that of her stealing Simon, or shoving him out of the tree or something equally dastardly. With a last, warning look, Jenn took off toward the back door and Megan waited until she knew Jenn couldn't hear her before she muttered a curse.

One that was promptly repeated by Simon.

"Nice, kid. You'll get me blamed for that, too, won't you? So what's the deal? You going to keep hugging that tree or come down? I could use a break about now." Maybe he'd come down and she could follow him inside.

Simon's face split into a curious half grin, his beautiful teeth shining even though a big fat tear dripped off his cheek.

"Tu m'apportes chez Dr. Ethan?"

Megan shook her head, her heart tugging at the tone the boy used. She knew that mix of hope and fear. She'd felt it when she'd finally broken her silence and talked to the E.R. nurse two years ago, wanting to trust that the nurse meant what she said about getting help and being safe from Sean, but afraid all the same.

"Sorry, but I can't take you anywhere, much less home," she told him in French. "Why don't you come down?" Before she fell down. Who knew facing Thumper could be so nerve-racking? Her legs had the consistency of jelly and if she moved too fast, everything wobbled like a drunk on a Sit-N'-Spin.

Simon flattened his back to the tree. *"Non."*

That "no" was very clear. Megan studied him for a moment. Simon's intelligence showed in his expressive eyes, but something altogether different was there, as well. Something wary and hard, something she recognized. While young, this kid was no pushover. And what was with the way he held so utterly still? No kid his age sat that still. No adult did, either.

Except the ones who knew the consequences of drawing attention to themselves.

Megan pressed a hand to her temple and rubbed. A low thump sounded somewhere in the neighborhood and the sound echoed off the houses. Seconds later a mower started from the other side of the fenced yard next door and sent birds squawking into the sky and her heart into overdrive. Damn, she had to stop being so jumpy. *"Simon, descends avant que tu tombes. S'il te plaît."*

After a long, hard stare from his golden eyes, the kid started a slow descent. Megan sighed. Finally. She wasn't sure what convinced him to mind her, but she wasn't about to question it.

Simon made it to the lowest branch. He dangled for a moment before letting go and dropped to the ground without incident. Two steps later he locked his arms around her legs and squeezed tight.

"Vas-tu rester jusqu'à ce que Dr. Ethan arrive?"

It took a moment for her weary brain to translate the words. Stay? If Simon wanted her to stay, she'd have to, right? Jenn obviously didn't want the kid upset. *Give you an inch and you take a mile.* "If you tell Miss Jennifer you want me to stay, she might let me."

Have you no shame?

Obviously not. And in the meantime, maybe Jenn would offer her something to eat and drink? Be a good hostess like ol' Martha would suggest? Then Megan could claim fatigue from her long drive and ask to lie down in a bedroom, just for a short nap. Surely Jenn wouldn't deny her that since she'd gotten Simon out of the tree?

Shameless. Absolutely shameless!

The boy took her hand. *"Es-tu malade?"*

Are you sick? Megan shook her head. She didn't have time to be sick and refused to admit defeat even though it felt like defeat was kicking her scrawny butt at the moment. She was chilled, aching, her headache growing worse. It was like her body had held on and functioned while it had to, long enough to get her here, but now it was tossing in the proverbial towel. *Yeah, that helps. Piss Jenn off more by making her sick.*

You're not sick. You're not sick. You're not sick!

"Tu as l'air mal. Pourquoi me mentes?" the boy promptly shot back, stating she looked sick and why was she lying?

Yeah, well, there was another sin. She was good at lying. She'd had to be to survive. *"Est-ce que tu vas prendre soins de moi si je suis malade?"*

The little boy nodded vigorously that he'd take care of

her if she was sick. "I'll remember that, kid," she murmured, wishing hopelessly that she and Jenn could talk as easily as she did with this boy. Wouldn't that be nice?

Simon made a noise in his throat, a French *uh-oh*, his eyes widening.

"What's wrong?"

"Simon! Simon, I told you to behave. Why have you been giving your aunt Jennifer a hard time?"

Expecting Jenn, Megan whirled to face the angry male voice, her heart in her throat because of the start it gave her and how she immediately thought Sean had found her.

It wasn't Sean. That much registered before she realized her body couldn't stop spinning once it was in motion. Her breath hissed out of her chest with a rough exhalation, and everything moved in Tilt-A-Whirl patterns. The sky, the grass, the house, the tree. All the colors blurred together in a big wave of distortion. Lost in the haze, she caught a brief flash of wide shoulders and dark hair before black circles blotted out everything but the pain of her body hitting the ground. She heard a disjointed moan and belatedly realized it was hers.

Hands touched her and rolled her over. She blinked and found Simon's panicked, wide-eyed face hovering above hers until a large, broad hand shoved Simon back with the order to give her some air. Stupid man, he'd said it in English, so she sluggishly told Simon she was fine in French and prayed her head wouldn't explode from the pressure inside it.

Why now? Why here? Another moan left her throat. Jenn would never let her in now.

"WHAT'S GOING ON, SWEETHEART? Come

on, talk to me. Are you diabetic? On any medication? Did you take any drugs?" Ethan stared down at the woman sprawled on the ground in front of him and wondered who she was. She had to be a friend or neighbor of his sister-in-law's for her to be in the backyard, but he didn't remember ever seeing her around Beauty.

"No," she whispered, wincing and lifting a shaking hand to cover her eyes. "No drugs. I'm…okay." She tried to sit up but only made it as far as her elbow. Ethan gently pushed her back to the ground and she went willingly, her trembling fingers moving to massage her temple.

"Somehow I doubt that." The woman was too pale, too thin, *gaunt*, if her hands and face were anything to judge by. Why was she so thin? Was she anorexic?

Her cheekbones were more prominent due to her extreme thinness, her nose, although perfectly shaped, was too big for her slender face. A surgeon himself, he focused on the slight scar visible only to the most critical eye. Maybe a little too perfect?

Ethan put his fingers to her throat. Her pulse was rapid but nothing dangerous, her skin clammy, her forehead much too hot. No wonder she was dizzy, she was burning up. If the thick sound of her breath was any indication, pneumonia was a definite possibility, bronchitis a given.

"Hey?" He ran his knuckles over her cheek when she stayed silent. "You with me?"

"I'm okay," she repeated.

Uh-huh. "Nice try but I have a feeling *okay* isn't something you're going to be for a while."

The hoodie she wore had ridden up and her jeans gaped at her waist, revealing the thin straps of a thong high on pointy hips. *Juicy* was stitched across her chest and with a little more meat on her, he would agree with the sentiment. But as it was, she reminded him a little too much of the women in Niger, all bones and skin and sunken eyes. Hers were a beautiful shade of blue-gray, but the purple shadows beneath made them look bruised.

Ethan ran his hands over her arm. She'd fallen hard but he felt no obvious signs of a break. He lifted her sweatshirt just high enough to slip his hand along her side to check her ribs. The sight of the sexy little glint of metal attached to her belly button sent his blood pressure soaring, despite the extreme inappropriateness of the moment.

Her entire body tensed. "Are you feeling me up?"

The comment caught him by surprise and a rough laugh left him. "No, I'm examining you."

"Well stop. I don't need some guy playing doctor."

He smiled, unable to help himself. "That's good because I'm not playing. I'm the real thing. Scout's honor. Want to hear my diagnosis?"

She eyed him suspiciously. "Not if you're going to charge me for it."

"This one's on me."

She lifted a shoulder in a shrug and winced at the move. "Go for it, then."

Ethan smiled down at her, amazed by her spunk when she was obviously aching. "You're very sick but you're going to live."

"Lucky me," she said wryly, her breath leaving her chest with a painful-sounding cough. "That means Jenn will have the advantage when she kills me."

Chapter 3

ETHAN WASN'T SURE what the comment meant but she didn't give him too much time to ponder the possibilities. She grabbed his wrist in a weak grip and held.

"You're almost at second base, you know. Another millimeter and you're either going to have a black eye or you'll have to buy me dinner."

A low chuckle left his chest and he shook his head. Taking one last look, he covered the temptation of her soft skin and readjusted her sweatshirt in spite of her fumbling fingers getting in the way. "No broken ribs but you do have some redness. You'll be sore tomorrow. How long have you been sick?"

"I'm not sick."

"You're not, huh?"

"Mind over matter." She breathed the words, the sound thick. "Can I get up now?"

"Pouvez-vous la guérir?"

Ethan's tired brain couldn't decipher Simon's question. "English, Simon."

The kid drew back at his tone and Ethan sighed.

Damn. He had to watch that, but patience was hard to come by these days, especially when he felt as if he was drowning half the time.

Simon's dark fingers slowly reached out and touched the woman's creamy forearm. The contrast between their skin tones was startling and denoted her paleness even more. She'd let herself get too run-down and hadn't taken care of herself in a while. The roots of her hair proved that. Her long brown hair didn't match the light blond at her scalp or her eyebrows. Most women he knew dyed their hair blond, not the other way around.

"Ethan, what are you—" Jenn's words broke off with a gasp. "What happened?"

"Oh, great," his patient murmured. "Help me up. Please, get me up." She sounded panicky.

Jenn was rapidly approaching them, a bright red Popsicle in one hand and the portable phone in the other. He grasped the woman's hand in his and felt her lack of strength. "Good timing. Your friend isn't feeling well."

"She's not my friend."

Ethan was taken aback by his sister-in-law's blunt declaration and the less than pleasant gleam in her eyes. "Excuse me?"

A deep, gusty sigh left Jenn's ample chest. "Ethan, my sister, Megan. Megan, Ethan."

"Move," Megan whispered, "and let me up."

Ethan stayed right where he was. "Not so fast. Just sit here for a minute until you get your legs back."

Jenn stared at them, emotions rolling over her face. Worry, upset. Anger. Anger was a big one, impossible to miss.

"What's wrong with her?"

He blinked once more, his eyebrows rising high because of Jenn's blatantly unsympathetic tone. Jenn hadn't been a member of the family long, but she was usually the ultimate in kindness and understanding. Who knew sweet Jenn had a dark side?

"She's burning up with fever and looks dehydrated," he told Jenn. "Megan, have you eaten today? Drank fluids?"

"This morning."

But nothing since? It was almost four in the afternoon. "I'll help you into the house." He put his arm around her too-slim waist and straightened, watching her closely as he brought her slowly to her feet. A second passed before her knees buckled, her face lost what little color it had regained, and even though she immediately righted herself by locking her knees and tightening her grip on his shirt, he caught her against him and swung her up into his arms.

"No, I'm all right."

"Ethan, don't. You'll hurt yourself." Jenn stepped toward them. "Put her down."

"My leg is fine." He bounced Megan in his arms to get a better grip and heard her teeth chattering. Poor thing. The fever was taking a toll on her. "Jenn, my bag is in the car. Will you get it?"

Jenn didn't look at all happy about the situation but he didn't care. Megan needed help.

Jenn handed the Popsicle off to Simon and turned on her heel to head around the side of the house. His newly adopted son shot him a questioning glance before Simon quickly looked away and lowered his head.

Ethan's guilt grew at the tone he'd used in talking to the boy. *"Simon, peut-tu ouvrir la porte?"*

Simon hurried toward the door to open it like Ethan had asked, but the boy stood there a moment as though unsure of what to do.

"Grab the left side and push it right." He waited impatiently, reminding himself that he and Simon had a long way to go and a lot to learn before they were comfortable with each other as father and son. Simon's early years had been spent in a tiny village in Niger where he'd lived in a hut pieced together from scrap wood and whatever else could be found. Simon's village might have spoken French, but the workings of a French door wasn't something Simon had learned there.

"It's okay, Simon, I'll get it. Sit out here and eat your Popsicle so you don't drop it on Aunt Jenn and Uncle Nick's carpet, okay?" He indicated the metal table and chairs on the patio and finally resorted once more to his deplorable French. "Stay here and eat the ice. *Here*, understand?" *Don't move and for pity's sake, don't run away*, he added silently.

Simon's head dropped in a nod.

Megan's weight was getting to him, slight though it was, and she was starting to mutter protests about wanting down. In rapid French she repeated his instructions to Simon, using a much gentler tone to address the boy while she glared at Ethan with her feverish eyes, her expression stating loud and clear she thought him an ass of a father. She'd have to join the club.

Juggling her and the door, he managed to open it far enough that he could shove his foot inside the crack and push it the rest of the way. The muscles in his leg screamed out a protest and pain shot all the way up to his hip. More proof that he wasn't ready to tackle the O.R. just yet. No way could he stand on the operating floor for hours at a time if he couldn't handle a short trip into the house.

He carried his patient across the kitchen into the living room to the couch and breathed a sigh of relief.

"I could've walked."

"Next time you can carry me," he countered, having a

hard time ignoring his throbbing leg. "Sit tight and we'll get you taken care of."

Jenn entered the house via the front door and hurried down the foyer hall with his black doctor's bag. Ethan grabbed his stethoscope the moment she set it beside him.

While he went to work he was aware that Jenn sighed, wrung her hands and sighed some more, in between stints of glaring at her sister and shaking her head back and forth like she had a conversation going on only she could hear.

Megan lay on the couch quietly, studiously ignoring Jenn.

"Breathe deep. That's it, deep breaths." The sweatshirt was too thick and he had to slip his hand beneath it. The move earned another tired yet sassy raised-eyebrow look from Megan. She appeared to be making an effort to rally her fighting spirit, but she wasn't up to it yet. He flashed her a grin. "Get well and I'll buy you that dinner."

Behind him, Jenn huffed.

Megan closed her eyes briefly, her lips quirking at the corners. Ethan listened closely, shifting the end of the stethoscope from her front to her back to check her lungs. Megan had definite congestion but no pneumonia. So far. "Bronchitis," he said aloud, unplugging the device from his ears. "And a severe bout of it from the sound of things." He slipped his hands to her jaw and neck to check her lymph nodes. Her skin was silky, her hair soft where it wrapped around his fingers. "You're exhausted. Any particular reason why?"

"I've been traveling a lot."

"That's no excuse not to take care of yourself." He continued the exam, taking her temperature last. "Fever is 103. You're one hot woman," he said for her ears only. The comment earned another weary smile, and he liked the way it lit up her eyes. "How long have you been sick?" he asked, focusing on the most pressing matter at the moment.

Ethan moved to the edge of the couch to relieve the pressure on his leg, and watched the ongoing silent byplay between the sisters. They glared at each other when they knew the other wasn't looking and avoided eye contact if they were. What was up with that?

Looking awkward, Megan dug her elbows into the cushions and struggled to push herself up. Ethan reached out and supported her while she repositioned herself against the sofa's back. "It...started last week. It's just a cold."

"Not anymore. The good news is that with rest, meds and food, you'll get better." Ethan waited for Jenn to back his words up with a supportive comment and was even more puzzled by her lack of response. This obvious dislike and upset with her sister was a surprise.

Jenn twisted her fingers together in front of her. "Megan, what are you doing here?"

It wasn't so much a question as an accusation.

"I was passing through and...thought I'd stop by."

Megan brushed her hair away from her cheek, her hand trembling visibly. When she caught him watching her, she lowered her hand and tucked it under her leg.

"That's it? All these years and now you're *stopping by?*"

Ethan shifted uncomfortably. He knew something of family dynamics, and experience told him he needed to get out of there while the getting was good, but—As he stared into Megan's face, his feet refused to budge. Something about her spirit, her spunk, the naked vulnerability she tried so hard to hide, kept him rooted.

"I know me showing up here is a surprise."

"You think?"

"Jenn." Megan said her sister's name in a way that both pleaded and coaxed. "Can we do this later?"

"Good idea," he said. "Megan needs to rest. While you get her settled, Simon and I will go get some antibiotics for her." He pulled a prescription pad out of his bag, almost missing the way Jenn blanched. He did a double take at Jenn's horrified expression. "What?"

"She can't stay here."

Ethan looked from Jenn to Megan and back to Jenn. "She's sick. Surely whatever this is between you two can't be that bad?"

Jenn opened her mouth but no words emerged. The look on her face said it all, however.

"It's fine," Megan whispered.

He split his attention between the two sisters, incredulous. "No, it's not fine. Whatever fight you two had doesn't matter right now. You're sick, and according to your tags, you came all the way from California to see Jenn. Everything else can wait."

Jenn lifted her chin. "I thought you were in Texas."

She didn't even know where her sister lived?

"I've moved several times since Sean and I divorced. You probably didn't know about that."

"Mom told me. He finally came to his senses?"

Megan's cheeks pinkened. "I left him two years ago."

"Well, you've obviously blown through the alimony in the meantime, judging by that heap of junk you're driving. Is that why you're here? You want money?"

"Jenn," he murmured, instilling a little more force into his tone. Maybe it was none of his business, but as a doctor, he had to step in. "Not now."

"I didn't take any of Sean's money in the divorce," Megan said softly. "I didn't want any ties to him."

Jenn shook her head as though she thought her sister's statement was a total lie.

Silence filled the room and Ethan continued to watch them. "Jenn, she's obviously not feeling well. Are you seriously going to stand there and kick her while she's down?"

Jennifer's face flushed at his rebuke. Having had more than enough drama, Ethan tucked the prescription pad into his bag and the slip of paper into his pocket but knew he couldn't leave until Megan was behind a door she could shut if things between her and Jenn got too bad. "You two can sort things out later. For now let me help you get her up to the spare bedroom so she can lie down."

"*No.* I mean…" Jenn huffed out a strained laugh, her hands fisting at her sides. "Megan, you can't just show up like this. You really want to stay *here?*"

Ethan noticed Megan had a hard time making eye contact, but she set her jaw at the raw emotion in Jenn's voice.

"Unless you don't want me to."

Jenn's face turned even redder when the challenge was thrown back at her. Obviously the two sisters didn't get along, but what did that matter when Megan was so weak she could barely stand? Megan couldn't travel like this, couldn't take care of herself. Couldn't Jenn see that?

Jenn remained silent, her mouth open as she took in shallow breaths, her expression making it clear she searched her mind for a viable excuse and battled tears while she did it.

Ethan stared at his peace-loving and typically agreeable sister-in-law, the one who taught classrooms of children and helped out at the hospital, the one who'd brought peace to his family by bringing Nick back into the fold, and knew he'd never understand women. Jenn was a total sweetheart but she'd help total strangers before taking in her own sister? What could've happened between them to cause such a rift? "What the hell is going on with you two?"

"It's just—It's complicated." Jenn's gaze pleaded for understanding. "Megan and I haven't spoken in years and…and it would be best if she stayed at a hotel."

Ethan purposefully didn't respond, giving Jenn time to ramble on.

"Megan did—She did horrible things and then disappeared. We haven't spoken since, but sometimes Mom and Dad wouldn't hear from her for years. Why is she here? Why now?"

"Why are you asking me?" He inclined his head toward Megan. "When she's sitting right there? This is your chance to talk it all out—after she's well."

"She can get well in a hotel."

Ethan pinched the bridge of his nose. Sweet Jenn wasn't budging, and even though he needed to go get Megan antibiotics, he was leery about leaving them alone. He didn't want Jenn ordering Megan out of the house and Megan attempting to leave, not as weak as she was.

Megan's chin lifted. "I won't stay long. I have a job. In Chicago. I thought I'd spend a few days here because—" she glanced at him and quickly looked away to where her hands gripped a pillow "—I just wanted to talk to you, okay? To apologize."

"Even if you apologize, you're not staying here. Megan, I don't trust you in my *living room*. Why on earth would you think I'd let you stay under the same roof as my husband?"

Chapter 4

THE TWO WOMEN glared at each other. Megan in sadness and extreme exhaustion, Jenn with disbelief. And fear? That crack about husbands...what did that mean?

An awkward silence filled the room and with every second that passed, Ethan became more convinced that he was surrounded by land mines. He should have left when he had the chance.

Jenn inhaled a shaky breath. "Megan, I'm sorry you're sick. I hope you feel better very soon and—and talking is fine. We'll meet up in a few days when you're feeling better."

He supposed under the circumstances that Jenn's offer was a concession on her part, but the sight of Megan lowering her head and swallowing hard struck a chord deep inside him. The sweep of her shoulder-length hair hid her face from Jenn but, sitting on the arm of the couch, he saw Megan struggle for composure. He couldn't stand seeing the expressions flicker over her face. Hurt, pain, disappointment. Defeat? He was treading water and drowning fast, but he couldn't let Jenn do this. This was

27

how his own family had been with Nick so many years ago. Didn't Jenn see that? Realize she was treating Megan the same way? People screwed up. And since Nick wasn't a two-timing kind of guy, Jenn had nothing to worry about.

"I'm sorry." Megan tucked her hair behind her ear, her gaze low. "I should've said it sooner, years ago, but…"

"But according to you, you never did anything wrong. Everyone else had the problem, not you—which is why I'm questioning this sudden reappearance and change of heart."

He waited, wanting Megan to speak up, Jenn to back off, or else one of them to say something more specific.

"Hey," Nick murmured from just outside the open glass door.

His brother stepped into the house and assessed the scene with one of his all-knowing glances, seemingly measuring Jenn's agitation and Megan's state of ill health in a matter of seconds.

Ethan had always envied Nick that ability. Some members of the family thought Luke was the sensitive one, the most observant, but Ethan knew it was Nick. After spending so many years as the outcast looking in, Nick knew how to read people better than anyone Ethan had ever known. And the fact that Nick hadn't barged in and immediately ordered Megan out said something.

Ethan released a breath he didn't know he was holding, relieved his brother had arrived. Getting involved in their sisterly squabble was the last thing he wanted or needed to deal with at the moment. Nick would calm Jenn down and help her see the right move to make, and he didn't have to feel guilty about leaving with Nick there to referee.

Nick walked over and greeted his wife with a brief kiss. Megan remained seated on the couch but, given her slow, precise movements, Ethan suspected she stayed put because she was still dizzy and perhaps even too weak to stand. Yet another reason for Jenn to cut her some slack until they were on equal footing.

Movement caught his attention and his gaze shifted to check on Simon's whereabouts. The boy's face was pressed up against the window, his chin sticky where it met the glass, eyes wide and fierce as he took in the scene. Simon looked ready to barge in to Megan's rescue.

Ethan wanted to tell Simon not to dirty the window but stopped himself in time. At least the kid was staying put. For now, anyway.

Turning to speak to Nick, Ethan paused when he saw Megan's lips curl at the corners in a brief smile when she saw Simon's face squished flat. She might not be Jenn's favorite person, but Megan had already conquered the toughest critic of all.

Nick stepped forward, hand extended. "I'm Nick, Jenn's husband."

Megan avoided Jenn's gaze. "Megan Rose. Nice to meet you, Nick."

Due to her illness, Megan's voice was throaty and deep and sexy as all get-out. Yet something else Ethan shouldn't be noticing, but he couldn't seem to help himself. Since coming home from Niger four weeks ago with Simon in tow, he hadn't had any female companionship. And he hadn't had the time or the interest to notice the lack until he'd glimpsed Megan's sexy little belly ring. Now it was all he could think about. Something about Megan brought out his own protective instincts—and his baser ones, too.

Nick ignored the tension and played it cool, and Ethan tried for that attitude, as well.

"You're not feeling well?" Nick asked.

"She's ill," Ethan heard himself say before either of the women could say Megan was fine and should be on her way. If Megan had the strength to walk out the door, he didn't doubt she'd do it. "Look, I'm going to get her the medication she needs so she can start on antibiotics before this turns into pneumonia."

"I'm not that sick. Really, it's just a bad cold."

Ethan shot Nick a grave stare. "She's this close—" he lifted his hand, his finger and thumb about an inch apart "—to needing hospitalization." Why wasn't she taking this more seriously? People died of pneumonia. "Megan needs meds, fluids and rest, and lots of it." He indicated the women with a nod of his head. "Good luck with that."

A DEAFENING SILENCE followed in the wake of Ethan's departure. Megan stayed where she was, lowering her head to rest on the cushions behind her because she didn't have the strength to hold it up any longer. She'd had the flu before, but she didn't remember ever feeling this bad. It was way distracting and scary stuff considering she'd driven to Tennessee like this. Thank God she hadn't hurt someone.

Megan forced her lashes up when she realized she'd closed them and found Nick whispering to Jenn. When Jenn simply glared back, Nick sighed and walked over to a rocking chair nearby. He grabbed the throw off the back and carried it to Megan. "Here. You want some tea? Jenn, why don't you fix—"

"No. Thanks, but I'm fine." She didn't want Nick ordering Jenn to fix her anything. If she read Jenn's expression right, her sister was waiting for Megan to jump up and climb Nick like a tree.

Which would be funny if it wasn't so sad. Sean had been her one attempt at doing the right thing, at protecting her little sister. Then her attempt at nobility had bit her in the butt.

She sank deeper into the cushions and pulled the throw over her lap and arms, aware that Nick had moved closer to Jenn to continue the quiet conversation she wasn't meant to hear.

"It's one night. Maybe two."

"No. Don't look at me like that. You know why, Nick. I can't believe you're taking *her* side."

"I'm not taking sides, but are you really going to send her to a hotel? Then what? Look at her, she's dead on her feet. How would she take care of herself?"

Their conversation ebbed and flowed, and Megan tried to open her mouth and argue that she'd taken care of herself so far and didn't need their help, but the words didn't come. The couch was soft and much more comfortable than her backseat, the throw nice and warm, even if she was still cold.

Her mind floated, back to one winter when it had snowed so much her recital had been canceled and her parents had taken her and Jenn to a cabin in the woods. She and Jenn had gone out to build a snowman to escape their parents' bickering and it had been freezing. She shivered just thinking about it.

That memory faded into another, this one darker, more frightening. Another snowy night, a party with too much alcohol. Loud music, the hot press of too many people in too little space and her determined to do the right thing for Jenn's sake. She'd known what Sean had planned to do with Jenn, known why the popular jock was dating her nerdy sister. She'd heard Sean bragging to his friends about how he was going to keep Jenn on the hook.

So Megan had set him up, wanting Jenn to see what a loser Sean really was because telling Jenn hadn't been enough. Jenn had called her a liar, refused to listen. But when it was over and Jenn had walked out, Sean had been furious. So furious he'd grabbed Megan and shoved her down. Held her down.

A whimper escaped her when she felt those large male hands on her now. They gripped her shoulders and shifted her sideways, pressing. Panic surged through her and when one of the hands moved to her legs—

Megan woke up with a shriek, kicking, punching, fighting with all her might. "No. *No!*"

"Dammit, ow, Megan, stop. Hey, it's okay. Megan, wake up."

The growled words pried the fog loose from her brain and she blinked, realizing too late where she was. Her heart pounded so fast it felt like it was going to burst out of her chest, and Nick now stood beside the couch, his hands palms up as he regarded her with eyes that saw too much.

"It's okay. Sweetheart, nothing's wrong."

"I'm not your sweetheart." She spat out the words, half sitting, half lying on the couch. What was he doing calling his wife's sister *sweetheart?* Touching her?

"I was just trying to make you more comfortable. You fell asleep sitting up."

The sore muscles in her neck said his words were true, but she still wondered if he'd used it as an excuse.

Not everyone is Sean. "You startled me." Hugging her arms around her stomach, she realized her teeth chattered and the chills were back.

"Yeah, I saw that. I brought you another throw. You said you were cold."

She had?

"I'm sorry I startled you."

Jenn came running into the room carrying a pillow. "What happened?"

Megan couldn't look at them. When the time was right she'd tell Jenn everything that had really happened in the past but not now. Megan glanced at Nick and found his gaze still locked on her, much too astute. Jenn's husband looked as though he may have been around the block a few times. Crap.

Stupid, stupid, stupid. "Nothing. I'm just really tired and your husband startled me. Maybe you're right. I need to sleep and you've got too many people around here. Maybe it would be best if I went to a hotel."

Jenn looked relieved and didn't that hurt?

"No."

"Nick, she said she wants—"

"She's not going anywhere."

AN HOUR AND A HALF LATER Ethan sighed as he settled himself into one of the reclining chairs in the living room beside Nick. The moment he'd returned with Megan's medicine he could feel the tension between Nick and his wife. Ethan wanted no part of it, but here he was still at the house and hesitant to leave. The last thing he needed was to take on responsibility for someone else, but how could he leave Megan behind with such an indifferent and antagonistic nursemaid as Jenn? "What the hell happened while I was gone?"

Nick sprawled in the soft leather chair, leaning an elbow on the arm and rubbing his hand over his mouth as he stared across the floor to the kitchen where his wife stood chopping up fruit like a chainsaw. "I informed them both that Megan was staying. She's family."

A reasonable dictate—if the circumstances were normal, which they apparently weren't.

Nick scowled. "How long until Megan's on her feet? I told Jenn it would only be a day or two."

Ethan winced.

"More?" Nick swore.

"At least until her fever breaks. Several days would be better, a week to ten days or until she's fully recovered would be best."

Nick muttered yet another curse, and Ethan echoed the sentiment, feeling his brother's frustration at being stuck between a rock and a hard place in doing the right thing and doing what would please his wife.

No one wanted to be hospitalized and, in Megan's case, she shouldn't have to be provided she had a place to stay and could keep the pneumonia at bay. But with Jenn upset over Megan's appearance, much less her presence, Megan was going to cause a heap of problems. *Just stay out of it. They're not* your *problems.* "Do I want to know what happened between them?"

Across the room, Jenn muttered to herself and went at a cantaloupe like a pissed-off chef. Every now and again, Nick's wife would lift her head and glare at Megan, even though Megan dozed on the couch, her face barely visible from beneath two blankets.

If she was out of it before, Megan was really woozy now that she had the prescription cold medication in her helping to alleviate her cough. Would Jenn make her sleep on the couch?

"They have issues."

"And you always were the master of understatement. I'd leave, but I'm afraid Jenn might use that knife on you the moment Simon and I are out the door."

Simon played with a ball on the floor. He sat with his

legs spread in a wide V as he rolled a ball gently across the floor where it hit the door and bounced back. Ethan knew enough to know any other kid would've been bored by the simple game but Simon's life made the kid easy to please.

"Eth, what would you think if you went to put a blanket over someone and tried to make them comfortable —" Nick shot him a look filled with tension, a muscle in his jaw flexing the way it did whenever Nick was angry "— and they screamed and came out swinging like a pro?"

Ah, hell. He'd think the same thing as Nick. Now he understood his brother's expression. Physical reactions like the ones Nick described came from fear. And fear like that came from being threatened.

Megan Rose might be trouble but everything in him shouted that she was *in* trouble. Financially, physically. Yet another reminder of Niger. So many abandoned families. Women left by husbands who either went off to find work and never came back or were killed in one of the many civil uprisings.

His worry over Megan kicked up another notch, as did his all-out fury. Someone had threatened her? Scared her that badly? How? What had they done? "What did Jenn say?"

"She wasn't in the room when it happened. By the time Jenn walked back into the room, Megan blew it off and made excuses, and Jenn was mad because I said Megan could stay."

So here Nick was stuck in the middle—and Megan stuck on the couch because Jenn was still trying to think of a way to get rid of her.

Ethan had seen Megan's car in the drive. He'd also noticed the pillow and blanket hidden in the back, but he hadn't paid too much attention to it due to his preoccupation with Simon's behavior. But now that he took another look at Megan and focused on Nick's comment, his suspicions gelled. The way Megan had appeared out of nowhere, her words to Jenn about her divorce, her reaction to Nick. Curses filled his head.

Damn, but he didn't need another person to worry over. Still, he couldn't help it. Megan would try to leave too soon just to be gone from where she wasn't wanted and move on to that job she'd told them about. "You can't think of a way to convince Jenn to let Megan stay long enough to get well?"

Ethan could see the debate going on in Nick's head, and he had to get out of there before he opened his mouth and said something he shouldn't. "Look, I hate to do this but I need to get Simon home. It's bedtime."

"Go. I'll handle this."

Ethan stood and made his way over to the kitchen counter, searching for something to say to make Jenn realize there wasn't really a choice to be made. "Jenn, I know this is hard, but she's family and she obviously has nowhere to go."

In an instant his sister-in-law's eyes overflowed and Ethan stepped back, appalled that his comment had earned that kind of reaction. Damn, damn, damn. He hated to see a woman cry. Jenn was Nick's bright, light, happy, easygoing, rarely angry wife. She wasn't someone to get upset over nothing. She was *that* upset about Megan being in her house? *She doesn't trust her sister alone with her husband. What do you think?*

"You have no idea what you're even suggesting. Don't you get it? I *know* how awful it is that I don't want my ill sister to be here, but I'd be an *idiot* to let her stay. I know her too well. You're looking at the outside but I *know* the inside. I know what she's capable of." The tears trickled down her face, and she wiped them away with the back of her hand, the knife flashing beneath the kitchen lights overhead as she waved it about to emphasize her point.

"Maybe she's changed. You said you haven't talked to her in years." He stepped closer. "Put that down before you cut yourself."

"I'm fine," Jenn insisted, sniffling. "It's just…I feel so *guilty*, but no woman in her right *mind* would welcome Megan into her home with her h-husband."

There it was again. And he didn't like the images his mind was coming up with at all. But who was he to cast stones given his past? Granted, he hadn't slept with any married women, but…"Fine, don't trust her, watch her like a hawk but at least let her get well."

"What about me?" Nick drawled quietly as he joined them. "That mean you don't trust *me* to be in the house with her? Do you think if Megan or some other woman comes on to me, I'll take her up on it?"

Ethan had never seen Nick look so pissed off. Aw, hell, things had just taken another downward spiral.

Jennifer wiped the last of the tears away and shook her head, but anyone watching could see that her effort lacked confidence. Her ex-husband had done a number on Jenn's self-esteem. Now it appeared as though Megan had, too.

"*No*. Of course I trust you. Nick, please. I don't want to fight with you. My point," she stressed, "is that Megan loves to play games. This proves it," she said with a wave of her hand in Megan's direction. "All of our lives she's used any situation to her advantage, now here she is doing it again. Yes, she's sick. But trust me, something's going on that she's not telling us. And I've learned the hard way to watch my back. Something's up with her, you mark my words. I'm sorry she's ill, I feel horrible, but I don't want her here, and neither one of you has the right to expect that of me."

Ethan grimaced. Unless something drastic happened, this situation was going to go from bad to worse because the tension kept escalating. Nick and Jenn's new marriage didn't need that.

"I, uh, guess I could take her home with me," he heard himself offer abruptly. Disgust rolled through him for giving over to the pressure he felt to fix things. Moron. "I'm not back to work full-time yet, and I heard her speak to Simon in French. She could…stay with me."

Jenn nodded, eager as all get-out. "She's fluent. Do you mean it?"

"It's a perfect solution." For them, anyway. "I don't go back to work full-time until the end of the week. Megan can crash at my house, get well and translate whenever Simon gives me that look because my French is so bad he can't understand me." He smiled with way more enthusiasm than he felt. "We'll be out of your hair in a few minutes."

Jenn dropped the knife and came at Ethan, barreling into his arms and giving him a hug. Nick's hand fell to Ethan's shoulder and squeezed in a show of thanks, but he noticed neither of them offered up so much as a squeak of protest.

Sucker. A list cycled through his head, all the things he needed to be doing instead of this. Ethan left Nick and Jenn and made his way to the couch where he stared at Megan's drawn, beautiful features. No doubt about it, he was already in over his head with Simon and here he was playing Dr. Fix-it. One of these days somebody really had to teach him how to say no.

He glanced over his shoulder and found Nick in the act of lowering his head toward Jenn's for a heated kiss. Ethan sighed. Didn't that figure? He was now responsible for a sick, potentially abused woman with a history of causing trouble and *Nick* was going to get lucky.

Ethan hefted Megan higher in his arms. A glint of shiny silver caught his attention and he glanced down, barely managing to stifle a groan at the sight of her sleek and sexy belly piercing. It was going to be a long week.

Because unprofessional or not, that was *hot*.

Chapter 5

MEGAN OPENED HER EYES, confused as to where she was when she didn't see the dome light of her Buick overhead or hear the steady roar of highway traffic outside the car windows. Instead, she was in an amazingly comfortable bed and not too far from where she lay, a night-light cast a glow from beside a bathroom sink.

Huh? She blinked and looked around the nicely furnished bedroom, her brain slowly kicking into gear with fuzzy images of the events leading up to this.

The pressing need to pee had her moaning a complaint. She so didn't want to leave the comfort and warmth of her covers, but she shoved them back and rolled to the right, her aching body protesting with pain and muscle soreness. As soon as she was upright she started coughing like crazy.

The bedroom door opened.

"Hey, where do you think you're going?"

Megan continued to cough and stared dazedly at the shadow of her host. A light burned behind him, making Ethan Tulane seem all the more imposing. Flirting with him was fine and dandy, but how smart was it to accept help from a total stranger? Stay in his house?

Like you had a choice? Jenn worked this out, not you. Besides, what can he do to you that Sean hasn't already done?

"Megan? You're not sleepwalking on me, are you?"

"No, I'm 'wake. I have to…" She waved a limp hand in the air toward the door on the far side of the room. "Bathroom." Was that her voice? She sounded like a bullfrog. A sleepy, grumpy, croaking bullfrog.

"Ah. Let me help you."

"I can do it."

"Okay. I'll stick around, in case you need a hand."

Never one to back down from a challenge when she heard one, Megan attempted to stand, but nothing worked the way it should. Her arms were too wobbly to give herself a decent push off the bed, her legs too weak, and her head whirled like a merry-go-round.

"Come on. I'll walk you to the bathroom and leave you alone, then help you back. Deal?"

She would've said no. No woman in her right mind wanted a stranger—a handsome doctor if memory served —helping her in to pee, but she really, really had to go and no way was she going to make it all the way on her own.

This was his fault. Her memories might be fuzzy, but she remembered enough to know Jenn's brother-in-law was responsible for waking her up to take medicine and drink gallons of fluids.

Even with Ethan's arm supporting her, her progress was pathetically slow, and by the time she reached her destination she felt as if she'd run a marathon. Once inside, Ethan shut the door and she was able to take care of business by collapsing onto the seat. Washing her hands required leaning against the sink for support, her energy zapped.

Ethan knocked softly before he opened the door. He took one look at her and swung her up into his arms to carry back to bed. She knew she should protest the move, but she was so grateful she didn't have to try to walk it that she kept her smart mouth shut and lowered her head to his shoulder, breathing in the scent of musk and man and—lemon-scented Pledge?

She squeezed her eyes closed to combat the dizziness when Ethan swung her around to lower her to the bed. This was what it felt like to be overcooked spaghetti. Even her brain was mush, a fact proven if she was smelling cleaning products instead of cologne.

Ethan tucked the blankets in around her waist then reached for the water bottle and pills on the nightstand. "Here. Time for another round. No arguing," he said when she opened her mouth to do just that. "They're keeping your fever down."

She swallowed the medicine and scooted down into a more comfortable spot in the bed. "What time is it?"

"Late—or early, depending on how you look at it. Around one. Go back to sleep."

Megan mulled that over for a second. She was tired, absolutely exhausted, but after all the activity she was also awake. "Can't. Maybe in a little while. Why are you awake?" The bed warmed her and took care of the shakes and chills she felt after being up and about. She probably looked like death warmed over, but she lacked the energy to do anything about it so why bother worrying? It wasn't like she wanted him or any other man to notice. She wanted to be invisible, needed to be to stay a step ahead of Sean.

Ethan lifted one hand to his face and rubbed harshly, the bristle on his cheeks rasping in the quiet room. "I'm a night owl. Are you hungry? I could heat up some of that soup I gave you earlier."

Sick or not, she sensed an evasive tactic. "Why can't you sleep?" She could tell Ethan wanted her to shut up, drop the subject and take the stupid soup, but she didn't want to. She needed a distraction in the worst way, something to keep her from thinking about Jenn.

Ethan capped the water bottle and set it aside. "Simon has nightmares."

Megan studied his face. She couldn't see Ethan well in the low light streaming in from the hall but she saw enough. Simon had nightmares, or Ethan? "What are they about?"

"Wouldn't you rather rest?"

"In a minute. Tell me."

Ethan leaned forward and braced his elbow on his leg. The pose was natural, casual, and it put her at ease even though he was so close. Strange, since she had a thing about personal space.

"I'd say he dreams of his homeland, the things he's seen. Simon cries in his sleep and sometimes…he wakes up and I find him huddled in a corner of his room."

Her heart ached at the image Ethan's words brought to mind. No wonder she felt a connection to the kid. "He'll tell you about them when he's ready. Sometimes it takes time to work up the courage to talk about things that scare you. Maybe he thinks you won't understand."

"Maybe. Now get some rest. Good night, Megan."

"Wait, don't go." She told herself to let him leave and mind her own business but something made her press. Maybe it was because Jenn wouldn't talk to her and she needed a connection with someone, maybe it was because she identified with the expression Ethan wore. Whatever the reason, she didn't want to be alone in the dark with only her thoughts and Sean's threats for company. "We'll talk about something else. Where is Simon from?"

Ethan made himself more comfortable at her side, a resigned sigh leaving his chest. "Niger. It's a long story."

Weren't they all? "Long-distance girlfriend?"

His teeth flashed once more. "No, nothing like that. I took an assignment with Doctors Without Borders and… came home with a son."

That was some souvenir. "What's your specialty?"

"I'm a surgeon."

"I'm impressed."

"You shouldn't be. It's a job, like any other."

O-kay. She plucked at the blanket and sheet, knowing she ought to be uncomfortable. But she wasn't. As her mind had noted earlier, there wasn't much Ethan couldn't do to her that hadn't already been done, and Ethan had a way about him that set her at ease. Weird.

Yeah, well, he's practically felt you up. That sort of thing has a way of upping the comfort factor. "That's not quite how most people view what you do. You know, what with the whole cutting people open thing going on. You don't like being a surgeon?"

"I don't like being made out to be more than I am." His rich, husky voice slid over her nerves like the softest of sand.

"Just because I do what I do doesn't mean I'm more important than anyone else."

Megan frowned, aware there was more to Ethan's comment than the obvious but not sure she wanted to pursue the subject given his mood and her growing awareness of him. It had to be the medicine kicking in. Why else would she be noticing his broad shoulders? The way his tone softened whenever he spoke of Simon?

But how many doctors, surgeons even more so, thought

they were God because they held life in their hands? But here Ethan was, different in his belief. A part of her acknowledged that it was a trait to be admired. Another wondered if he was for real.

Her host shoved himself off the bed and stood. "You need to rest."

She shifted on the pillow. "Why did you sign up with Doctors Without Borders?"

He hesitated a long moment and she could feel Ethan studying her in the light of the hallway.

"I made the decision to sign up after I'd been turned down for a promotion. I thought it would be nice to go somewhere where I could do some good and get back to the reason I became a doctor in the first place."

"And let whoever passed you up choke on their mistake?"

"Why not? They made a bad decision."

Why not indeed? Who wouldn't want that kind of satisfaction? "Have they choked?"

"Yeah. The guy's a lousy chief of surgery. The problem is that he's now my boss and there's nothing I can do about it unless I want to practice somewhere else."

"Ouch. So you went to Niger. Did you like it?"

A slow, one-sided smile pulled at his mouth. "I loved it, although I wasn't prepared in the least."

"Prepared for what?" She'd learned to look beneath the surface during her time with Sean, watch for clues to his mood. Ethan was tired, maybe more exhausted than she was. Frustrated but calm. Still, here she was keeping *him* awake. Maybe she ought to let him go and not expect Ethan to entertain her.

"I thought I knew what I was getting into, but I didn't count on meeting up with rebel forces."

Whoa. "Seriously?" The warmth of him seeped

through the blankets and into her side where he sat next to her, reminding her that he was here and alive so all had turned out well. Thank God. On a purely selfish level, what would she have done if he hadn't made it back?

"The organization is fantastic when it comes to protecting their people, but some things are out of their control and can't be helped. You know that going in. Some days are peaceful, some not. Eventually you wind up on edge, waiting for the next round because you know it's coming. While I was there things got heated and it became a matter of when something would happen, not if."

Images came to mind, her nightmares. The taunts and slurs and memories she tried to keep buried. A matter of when, not if, just as he'd said.

"Is something wrong?"

She'd tensed without meaning to. "No," she said softly, pulling herself from the past and unclenching her fists from the blanket. "No, go on. What was it like?"

He hesitated a fraction of a second. "Beautiful. Terrifying. Medicine is in short supply. What they receive gets raided periodically by the guerillas and everything is rationed, even though the patients suffer for it."

The sound of Ethan's voice soothed the tension that filled her. She watched him, admiring Ethan's dedication that he'd do something like that, take that kind of risk, and yet wondering why. Why go? Why volunteer? Was it brave, or stupid? In today's world, why would someone who had a job and a house, a great career, risk it all?

Maybe because Ethan doesn't think only of himself? If he did, you wouldn't be here.

Maybe. And that was great; the world needed more people like Ethan. But she wondered if there was more to it. She couldn't help but think people like that, people able to do those types of things, had never known true, life-and-death fear. Gut-knotting, heart-in-your-throat terror where you wonder if the end is a breath away. If they had, she believed most wouldn't volunteer to go face more of the same. "How did you meet Simon?"

Ethan speared his fingers through his hair and raked the short strands back. "Word reached the camp that a group of children were trying to make their way to us."

"Alone?"

"They'd started off with a couple of their teachers, but the adults had either abandoned them or died trying to protect them from the guerillas in pursuit. Simon is—was—my translator's nephew. Isa had already lost his sister to AIDS a year earlier and he didn't want to lose Simon to the fighting."

Her brain focused on one word—AIDS. "Was Simon infected by his mother?" The shock of it gave her pause. After leaving Sean, she'd moved around quite a few times. But in every city she'd made a point of going to the support groups and counseling classes held at the shelters. She'd read the pamphlets and attended the free meetings on domestic violence and she knew the statistics.

"No. But the spread of the disease is one of the many reasons Isa asked me to bring Simon home as my son. Isa wanted Simon to be in a safer place, one where the meds are available if Simon ever needs them, where he wouldn't be kidnapped and forced to fight." Ethan rubbed his palm over his eye. "Simon's tested negative for HIV twice already. He'll have another test in six months, but it's more of a precaution since the first two were negative."

She thought of Simon's sweet little face, pictured his huge honey-colored eyes. Innocent, and yet old beyond his years. "Simon's here with you because his uncle didn't make it." Ethan gave her a slow nod, his expression so tormented a lump appeared in her throat. "I'm sorry."

"Me, too."

Her heart stalled in her chest when Ethan lowered his head. She was more than ready to drop the subject now but Ethan made no effort to walk away.

"We went after the kids. We had to because—If the rebels found them first, they'd force them into their army. It's their standard recruiting procedure," he explained, his tone taking on a lethal dose of disgust. "Their so-called army is filled with children, some of them not even in puberty, carting around machine guns because if they don't, their family members are murdered as punishment."

She covered her mouth with her hand. Poor little Simon. He must have been so terrified. Thank God Ethan *had* gone after them, that there were men left in the world who'd protect those who couldn't protect themselves.

"I pictured Matt, Nick's son, in the same situation. He's nine. No kid deserves that kind of life."

Jenn had a nine-year-old stepson? Once more her heart stuttered and stopped. Megan quickly slammed closed the mental gate about to release the flood of anger inside her. So many regrets, so many wishes. She couldn't think about it, couldn't allow herself to consider possibilities that no longer existed, of what she'd lost. If she did, if she didn't keep those thoughts locked away, she couldn't breathe because her arms felt so empty, the pieces of her shattered heart cutting like glass. How would she ever move forward?

By outsmarting Sean and disappearing for good.

Focusing on Ethan rather than the things she couldn't change, Megan reached out and tentatively touched his hand, stroked her fingertips over the bumpy, lightly chapped knuckles. She hurt for him and the loss of his friend, recognized the anger and the horrific sense of useless waste.

"The rebels caught us. They typically left the base

49

camp alone because the hospital had treated several of their members. The camp heard the gunfire and the guards came to help, and we found ourselves stuck in the middle."

She pictured the scene, the chaos. "How old were they?"

"None of them were over eleven."

Her hand tightened on his, pulled it closer until she held him against her waist, hugging him to her. "Simon?"

"He was one of the youngest. He probably would've been killed or else kept for a slave or entertainment until he was older." Ethan swore softly. "The girls were crying. They knew what would happen to them if the rebels got hold of them."

"Oh, those poor kids."

He looked up, his gaze meeting hers. "I shouldn't be telling you this, at least not now. This isn't exactly a bedtime story."

His hand rolled beneath hers, until they were palm to palm, his thumb stroking oh-so gently over her skin. Surprise surged at the flash fire the simple caress sent spiraling through her, but she didn't fight it. Her instincts were hard-earned and honed by Sean's fists, and in that moment it felt nice to be touched by a man. "I don't need bedtime stories." The rasp of his skin against hers sent a shiver through her. "I'm not a child. Whatever happened…it won't scare me."

"And why is that?"

He'd lowered his voice to match hers, the darkness surrounding them cozy.

"What happened to you, Megan? What really brought you to Beauty? Was it Jenn and whatever's going on between you two, or something else?"

Chapter 6

ETHAN HADN'T MEANT TO PUSH Megan for answers until she was better, but he couldn't help it. Still, he regretted the questions when she pulled her hand away. The light from the hall let him see her tense features, assuring him he'd pushed too far, too fast.

Megan shifted away from him on the pretense of snuggling more deeply into his bed and the sight stalled him. Even sick she drew his interest. And the sight of her there? Virtual stranger or not, she just seemed to fit.

Something about the way she looked at him compelled him to share memories he hadn't been able to verbalize except in the most basic way to his family and colleagues. Maybe if he told her about his past, what he'd been through, she'd share more of her life before coming to Beauty? It was worth a shot, especially since his impression was that once she was well, Megan's guard would be up and she'd only share what she chose. "I'll tell you mine if you tell me yours."

That earned a small smile. "My what?"

"Your story."

"What's to tell? Look, all I'm saying is that anyone can see Simon isn't a normal kid. He's old beyond his years. I noticed that as soon as I saw him. He was up in the tree at Jenn's and…he sat so still."

She had no reason to trust him. Maybe in time she would. "They learn at an early age that if there's trouble they need to disappear if they can."

"But if they can't?"

Her gaze swallowed him whole and Ethan felt himself getting sucked into the warmth and tenderness and wariness he saw in her eyes. It wasn't as disconcerting as it probably should've been. "They also learn to fight."

"Is that what you did? When the rebels found you?"

"We had to. We were pinned down, stuck between the gunfire."

"Were any of the children hurt?"

He heard their screams in his head, the deafening quiet when it stopped. "Physically they only had superficial wounds. But emotionally?" He was having nightmares and he hadn't been through half of what the kids had gone through. He could only imagine…

"What happened to Isa?"

He stood and moved away from the bed, unable to sit still. He didn't have to tell her, but at the same time he wanted to. "When it looked as though the hospital guard had won, we moved toward the base camp again. One of the rebels came out of nowhere." In his head the man's image appeared, black eyes glazed, the evilest of smiles. All of eighteen, the killer had been high on drugs and the rush of murdering innocents. "He laughed and said something about taking the kids another way." He braced his fist on the wall, his blood pumping through his veins fast enough to cause a roar in his ears. "He pointed the gun at me and

Isa…. Isa jumped in front of me as the guy pulled the trigger."

"He took the bullet for you?"

With the image replaying itself in his head, Ethan hit the wall with his fist. The force of it rattled pictures, but he regretted his temper when Megan inhaled sharply and he turned to see her looking around as though ready to bolt from the bed for a safe place to hide. "I'm sorry. I didn't mean to startle you. I just…I see it. In my head. I see Isa doing that and I can't stop it."

Her expression softened at his words; the fear disappeared and was replaced by understanding. "You see it over and over again, don't you? Like a bad dream you can't wake up from. I know how…how frustrating and upsetting it can be."

"I'm sorry I scared you."

"Hey, don't worry about me. The medicine is just making me jumpy."

Her hair stood up at all angles; the old football jersey he'd given her to wear swallowed her and made her look ten years younger than she was, and she sounded like her throat was raw, yet he'd never seen a more appealing woman.

You're horny. She's Jenn's sister, remember?

"Ethan? Really, keep going. Tell me all of it. Please. Where was he—Where was Isa hit?"

Where wasn't he? "Everywhere. I might have been able to save him if there had been a single shot but—Isa was hit at least a dozen times. One bullet grazed my leg but Isa took the rest."

Her hand was over her mouth again. He fought the urge to rejoin her on the bed and pull her into his arms, whether it was to comfort her or himself he wasn't sure.

"I don't know what to say. I can see the guilt on your

face, but you didn't ask him to protect you. Isa made the call. It was his choice, not yours."

As soon as the words emerged from her mouth Megan frowned, her eyebrows furrowing in a contemplative expression as though considering them in regard to something else.

"That doesn't change the fact that he shouldn't have died for me. He was still conscious. Bleeding out. I asked him why and he said—" Covered in sweat and dirt and blood, Isa's face appeared in Ethan's mind, along with the kindness and hope in the man's eyes as he'd bled to death. The lump in Ethan's throat grew until it was hard to speak. "He said my life was more important, that the sacrifice of one for many was an honor and one of love for his people."

Megan was looking his way, but he doubted she could see much in the darkness. Given the burning in his eyes, he was glad she couldn't. "How do I not feel guilty that a good man gave his life for me?"

She made a sympathetic sound. "You shouldn't feel guilty because Isa did what he wanted to do," she said softly, her voice low. "What he felt he had to do. And I think—" she glanced down, her fingers twisting the material of the sheet "—if it came down to it, I—Isa would do it again."

Maybe it was his imagination but he could have sworn she'd said *I* and changed it to *Isa*. What sacrifice had she made? In regard to Jenn?

"You look exhausted. Why don't you go to bed and try to rest. Maybe talking about it helped some."

"Maybe." Turning, Ethan retraced his steps to the door. Megan looked so small in the bed, all eyes and dark hair and pale, pale skin. Fear and sadness, stoic vulnerability. He had to find out what her sacrifice had been. Why she'd done it, who she'd sacrificed for.

"Good night, Ethan. Thanks for letting me stay."

His grip tightened on the doorknob. "Good night."

After leaving Megan's room, Ethan checked on Simon, swearing softly when he found the boy lying on the floor instead of in the bed. Simon twitched and flinched in his sleep, his forehead wrinkling at whatever image his mind held.

Ethan debated whether to return Simon to the bed or let him be. The past couple weeks had proven that Simon just got back on the floor after Ethan left the bedroom, so he grabbed the blanket and covered the sleeping boy.

Sweet dreams for a change, buddy. Sweet dreams.

Straightening, Ethan rubbed his neck, exhausted. The talk with Megan had brought back gut-churning memories. Painful regrets. Isa had begged him to give Simon a good life, but how could Ethan give Simon anything when the boy was so distant? Simon obviously wasn't adjusting to living with him. They'd been in Beauty four weeks, together every day. But they'd made little to no progress. What would it take? Simon was as distant as the day of Isa's death. Did Simon blame him for what happened? Think he should've died instead?

Ethan headed back to the living room to straighten up, but nothing was out of place. Books were put away in the bin, crayons stored, pillows neat. The coffee table and side tables gleamed with polish.

He entered the kitchen, searching for something to occupy him and take his mind off his thoughts. Sometimes if he was exhausted enough he got a few hours of sleep in before the nightmares began.

The kitchen was clean, not even a crumb on the floor.

Restless, he pulled out a rag anyway.

"SIMON, DON'T JUST sit there. Eat."

Megan made her way toward the sound of Ethan's voice, feeling like a bus had hit her. How long had she slept?

Long enough for someone to get your suitcase.

"Simon."

Jeez, what was Ethan's problem? After their late-night talk, she would've guessed him to be a little more patient. He certainly seemed heroic with his jaunts to Third World countries and rescuing orphans and strays like herself. Barking at the kid wasn't the way to get Simon to eat or do anything else. She ought to know. When her parents or Jenn had yelled at her, she'd done the opposite of what they'd wanted, just to piss them off.

Not every kid is as stubborn as you.

Megan made her way through the living room slowly, her fingertips smoothing over walls and furniture because her balance still wasn't what it should be and her legs felt like someone had removed the bones and replaced them with goo.

She'd washed her face and found her toothbrush in her suitcase, but her hair was a mess of tangles nothing short of a shower and good conditioning would get out. She didn't have the energy to deal with that now. Ethan and Simon would have to get used to her bedhead.

Water ran and dishes clanked together. She followed the sounds but paused outside what she assumed was the kitchen door, unease filling her even though she wasn't sure why.

The living room was decorated with a plush leather

couch, coffee and side tables, a couple recliners and a cherry dining table with matching chairs. A big-screen television took up most of one wall and hung over a fireplace. But other than a few photo frames atop the mantel and pictures on the wall, absolutely nothing cluttered the room. The floor was clean—the vacuum marks visible—and not a speck of dust could be seen.

So he's got a great housekeeper. Good for him.

She walked over to the window facing the street and peeked out from behind the blind, noting the neighbors' cars and looking for anything suspicious. Maybe it was the room and its neatness but she was on edge. Would Sean think to come to Tennessee?

Stop worrying. Give it a rest already.

She glanced at the room once more, the knot in her stomach growing. Sean had had a thing about clutter. No knickknacks, no magazines, no baskets or pretties. Nothing to make a home feel like a home. The cold medicine made her woozy and disoriented. Who's to say it hadn't taken the edge off her instincts where Ethan was concerned?

"Simon, it's getting cold. Eat."

Forcibly shoving her thoughts aside, Megan reminded herself that not all guys were like the husband in *Sleeping with the Enemy*. Not all were Sean. And a busy guy like Ethan hired stuff out. Bachelors weren't known for being domestic, right? Nor were they known for having pretties lying around.

She took a fortifying breath and made her entrance into the kitchen where the man in question stood washing dishes at the sink, his shirtsleeves rolled up to his elbows. Ethan turned when he heard her and her already weak knees threatened to buckle.

Well, crud. Now she wished she had mustered the

energy to shower, but since he'd seen her at her worst, she'd considered herself safe. What a crock.

She remembered dark hair and a heck of a smile, she even remembered him striking her as somewhat handsome, but had Ethan Tulane always been so gorgeous? She didn't remember *that*. She'd felt so bad at Jenn's that she truly hadn't paid any attention but…*helllllo, doctor*.

Chapter 7

ETHAN HAD A DIMPLE in his left cheek that flashed when he smiled a greeting at her. It was amazing what that did to soften his too-chiseled features. Amazing what it did to her insides, sick though she was. It was too bad he was such a grouch because the man was seriously lethal on the senses.

And huge. Something else she apparently hadn't noticed. She didn't like big men, and Ethan towered a good six inches over her five-eight. He wasn't overly muscular, but lean and long and lanky, dressed in faded blue jeans and an untucked white shirt, his large hairy feet bare. She'd always considered brains sexy and humility a turn-on, but the two together in an I'm-a-surgeon-but-I'm-just-a-man package was downright toe-curling.

"Hey, you're up," Ethan said, his smile growing wider. "How do you feel?"

A list of words ran through her head, none of them appropriate for children. "Alive." She glanced at Simon, a smile at the ready, but the boy didn't look up.

Ethan gestured toward the table. "Sit down and I'll fix you something to eat."

She eyed the kid's plate. Whoa. No wonder Simon wasn't smiling—or eating. "Um…I'd love some coffee."

"You've haven't eaten anything but soup for days. You need real food."

Megan blinked, taken aback by his words. "What do you mean, days?"

"It's Wednesday. You ran a high fever when you arrived on Monday, but it broke early yesterday morning. You've been sleeping ever since." Ethan grabbed a towel to dry his hands. "Let me give you my doctor speech and get it over with, okay? Don't ever let yourself get that run-down again. Exhaustion is serious when you're dealing with your immune system. You made it to Jenn and Nick's just in time. I doubt you would've made it any farther without causing an accident."

She lowered herself into a chair opposite Simon. *Days?*

"Simon, did you say hello to Miss Megan?"

The unhappy kid still stared at the food on his plate. Poor thing. That was a lot of charcoal. What was Ethan trying to do, incinerate it? "You two have been taking care of me all this time?" Where was Jenn? Didn't she care at all? Had she come by? Was she the one who'd brought her suitcase over?

What do you think? If she had to guess, she'd bet Ethan picked it up for her or else grabbed it out of her car that first night.

"Simon's a good helper. He listened for you in case you called out and needed something while I got some work done." Ethan set a dish aside and grabbed another. "It worked out fine."

Fine? Megan lifted a trembling hand and fingered a

tangle in her hair, wishing she'd at least taken the extra time to brush it out. *"Merci, Simon."* She made eye contact with Ethan and gave him a weak smile. "Thanks for all the help."

"No problem." Ethan turned back to the stove and lifted the pan for her perusal. "Would you like some eggs?"

Those were *eggs?* "Oh, um, no, thank you. Maybe just some toast?"

"Coming up." He grabbed the bagged bread and stuck two slices in the toaster.

Easing into the chair, Megan studied Ethan's movements. He had a limp from the bullet wound he'd received in Niger, but he tried not to favor that leg. If anything he put more weight on it, as if he was testing it and was determined to speed the process.

"I know you want coffee but we also have milk, orange juice, cranberry-apple juice—"

"Just coffee. It smells wonderful." At least he hadn't burned it.

"Fine, coffee *and* juice. You need the vitamins."

She sat quietly while Ethan puttered around the kitchen and tried not to focus on the way he cleaned and scrubbed everything in sight. On the one hand it was great. What was it about guys doing domestic chores that was so sexy? She supposed after having waited on so many men— a large portion of them ass-grabbing jerks—in the high-end restaurants and resorts where she typically worked, she liked having someone wait on her for a change.

But on the other hand, there was something about his movements that gave her that tingly, what's-up-with-this feeling again, like it wasn't about the cleanliness of the room. The kitchen was as spotless as the rest of the house but Ethan kept on scrubbing.

Stop it, already. Maybe Ethan and Sean have similarities but you're being ridiculous. Get up and help and stop jumping to conclusions.

"You need to take it easy today. If you're sore, a dose of ibuprofen should take care of the pain."

Now that he mentioned it, her legs and back ached and she had that weak-jittery feel you get after you exercise too much. "Thanks. I'll do that after I eat and shower. I feel like a stale gym sock."

The dimple flashed again. "That was the fever. You can take a quick shower, then it's back to bed and more rest."

You can take a quick shower? "Are you always this bossy?"

The complaint slipped out before she could stop it and Megan waited for the fallout. How rude. Sean's mouth would've pinched into that line that said he was angry and then he would've come over to her with a tight smile on his handsome face before he set out to show her exactly who was boss.

But Ethan—She blinked when her comment brought out a full-fledged smile and chuckle that eased the tension on his face. He wasn't angry his rude houseguest couldn't keep her mouth shut?

"Just being cautious. You might be feeling better, but you're still sick. I don't want you to overdo it too soon."

Oh. She relaxed, a tad. *See? Not Sean.* "Thanks. I won't overdo it. I'm not a person to just sit around, though, you know? I hate being sick. And let me say now that I appreciate your letting me stay here and taking care of me. Truly."

"So you've already said. It's not a problem. Do you know how long you plan to be in town?" He held up his hand. "Let me clarify that. I'm not asking you to leave or indicating you should, merely curious. You're welcome to stay until you're well and you and Jenn have made up. You're using the spare bedroom so you're not putting anyone out."

She tugged at the end of the jersey he'd given her to wear when they'd first arrived and realized it made her feel like a schoolgirl again, not a time of her life she wanted to revisit. "That's, um, very generous of you, but if I stay until Jenn and I work things out, I might be here forever."

Ethan's dimple reappeared. "The point I was trying to make is that you don't have to be in a rush. You need time to recover. I don't expect you'll have the energy to get back on the road for a while yet."

Back on the road…Her *car!* Either Ethan or Nick had been in her car. Had she had the sense of mind to move the blanket and pillow in the backseat? She couldn't remember.

Ethan drummed his fingers against the countertop and Megan found herself studying him more closely. Nick and his brother shared the same black hair and sharp features, but she remembered Nick looking…larger, more brutish. Ethan was just as tall but he appeared to be a kinder, gentler version. Ethan's profile was sharp, distinctly defined with a longish nose that had been broken at least once, a strong chin and a dusting of morning stubble on his cheeks.

Sexy, very sexy. Not that she was interested. Sticking around wasn't really an option.

The best-case scenario would've been for Jenn to forgive her and ask her to stay for a little while, but she knew that was asking for the moon. Jenn wanted Megan nowhere near Nick. How could she convince Jenn she wasn't here to cause trouble?

Maybe by finally telling her the truth?

But what about the strange car following her in Dallas?

Or the guy asking about her in San Francisco? She'd changed jobs three times there and he'd shown up every time. No, there had been too many coincidences, things she couldn't ignore. "Yeah, well, maybe Jenn will talk to me soon and then you and Simon can turn this place into a bachelor pad again."

"Ça va mieux?"

Megan's attention was snagged by Simon's lyrical little boy voice. "Yes, Simon. Much better. Thank you for asking."

Out of the corner of her eye, she saw Ethan's head turn, but before he could comment the telephone rang.

Ethan picked up a portable handset and glanced at the face. "It's the hospital. Would you mind watching him for a few minutes?"

"Not at all. We'll be fine." The moment Ethan was out of the kitchen, she turned to Simon and nudged his plate. "I wouldn't eat it, either. Would you like something else?" she asked in French.

Simon looked more than a bit apprehensive but nodded hesitantly, his gaze flicking to the door. Anger filled her. She knew that look. She'd worn it too many times herself not to recognize it. Fear, unease. Leeriness of making someone bigger and stronger angry.

"Simon? The food is burned. It isn't edible. It's okay to say you don't like it," she told him, wrinkling her nose and sending a disgusted look at the plate.

Simon lowered his head and mumbled something that sounded like, "Dr. Ethan made for me. I eat."

Getting a fresher, newer whiff from the toaster, she got to her feet and hurried to the appliance, popping the bread up just in time. Only a little crisp and she could scrape off the edges. Did the guy have a thing for carcinogens? What was the deal with burning everything?

Conscious that Simon watched her, she lowered the setting, grabbed the bagged bread and put two more pieces in, pushing the lever down with a defiant little *click*. Determined to give Ethan the benefit of the doubt for his earlier grumpiness with Simon because the guy was under a lot of pressure from all sides, she tossed Simon a reassuring smile and earned a shy one in return. "Simon, Dr. Ethan wouldn't want you to make yourself sick. He's a bad cook," she said, winking as though sharing a secret. "I'm not too hot at it myself, and that's okay. I'm sure Dr. Ethan did his best. But it doesn't mean…It doesn't mean we'll be punished if we say we don't like it. We're *allowed* to not like it."

The toast popped up and she quickly buttered it, adding a little of the strawberry preserves she found in the refrigerator.

Minutes later Megan was glad she'd gone foraging in the fridge because it was so cute the way Simon's eyes lit up when he tasted the preserves. They looked to be homemade and were probably full of sugar, but they tasted wonderful. So much so she made them each two more slices of toast topped with the gooey, delicious fruit.

Licking fingers free of sugar and sharing secret grins, she asked Simon about his favorite things to do. Getting answers out of the child was like pulling teeth, but before they were finished, Simon was smiling and nodding when she phrased her questions the right way, and Megan realized she was worn-out. Her stomach was full but instead of a shower all she wanted was to crawl back into bed. What was taking Ethan so long? She didn't want to leave Simon unsupervised.

"Come on," she murmured after washing their plates and chugging Simon's original breakfast down the disposal.

"Let's go plant ourselves in front of America's favorite babysitter."

And while Simon settled down in front of the television, she could check out the window one more time. Better safe than dead.

WHEN ETHAN EMERGED from his bedroom he found Megan asleep on the couch and Simon snuggled beside her, wide-eyed at the sight of Jerry beating the daylights out of Tom. He'd limited Simon's TV watching so as to not overexpose him, but Megan obviously didn't know any better—and was so exhausted she'd needed an extra hand in entertaining the boy.

"Do you like it?" he slowly asked in French, tongue twisting as he stumbled over the words.

Simon looked up at Ethan from beneath his long lashes then quickly looked away.

Ethan sighed. He'd thought a month would be enough time to get Simon settled and comfortable, but the boy seemed to be withdrawing more day by day, going in the opposite direction Ethan needed Simon to go.

He'll come around, give the kid time. That's what the counselors said, what the day-care manager had said both times he'd had to go to the hospital-based facility to pick Simon up early. And at Jenn's…

How could Simon run away from day care and throw such a fit at Jenn and Nick's, yet act so remote and removed when they were together?

Sighing, Ethan bent and gently shook Megan's shoulder. "Megan? Megan, come on, let's get you back to bed."

She smiled a slow smile that punched him in the gut

and sent his blood coursing through him, her long lashes fluttering open sleepily.

"That's what all the boys say."

Reining himself in, he tugged her to her feet. "I'll bet they do."

Chapter 8

ETHAN STARED DOWN at the worn piece of paper he'd pulled from his pocket, the ink from his latest notation drying in front of his eyes. His list of attributes he wanted in a wife, when and if he ever found one, was a source of amusement for his family, but the list served as a reminder of the things he found appealing and kept him from focusing on the surface aspects and carnal responses a guy felt when faced with sex on heels. A good body turned a guy on but a woman with a good body and a sense of humor? That was sexy.

How was it that he'd missed listing that quality until now? Megan's sense of humor came out at the oddest times, catching him off guard and making him laugh. Like yesterday when he'd pulled her to her feet off the couch. Her comment had not only earned a chuckle, but it had made him hot for her in a totally unprofessional way. And he liked it. A lot.

Jenn would no doubt kill him if he got tangled up with her sister, but if Megan Rose was as intriguing when she was well and healthy as she was when she was sick, it might be worth the tongue-lashing he'd get.

Tucking the list back into his wallet, he finished up his notes on Mrs. Darlington's chart, upset with himself and his leg's healing progress. His first surgery since coming home from Niger had gone well, but the short, sixty-minute procedure was nothing like those he'd have to perform on a regular basis. As it was, his leg throbbed.

He glanced at his watch and frowned. He should've been home two hours ago. When she'd called about Simon he'd told Jenn he'd be back by ten this morning, begging, pleading and promising her that Megan would sleep late and Jenn wouldn't have to see her sister if she'd take Simon home to familiar surroundings. But here it was nearing eleven and Ethan wondered how many calls Nick had received from Jenn to come save her.

"I hope you're not in a hurry to leave."

Ethan looked up to see Jonathan Morrow walking toward him. The fifty-something man had been appointed by the board as the new hospital president after the takeover had forced the former president into retirement.

The hospital had merged with a Nashville-based university hospital at the beginning of the year, but apparently the board hadn't been pleased with the former president's decisions. Ethan hadn't been pleased with them, either. Harold Pierson was the one who'd given the promotion of chief of surgery to a doctor with more attitude and ego than skill, so in Ethan's opinion, the changeover was a good start for things to come.

"Mr. Morrow," Ethan greeted, holding out his hand to greet the man, careful not to limp or show signs of pain. Any hesitation on his part that he wasn't ready to return to the O.R. would be noted and discussed by the board, and he had no intention of giving them any ammunition. "What are you doing down here on the floor?"

"Looking for you. First surgery since you've been back, eh? It went well?"

"Yes. The patient is resting comfortably." If only he was.

"Good, good." The man flashed Ethan a smile. "But I'm sure you know that's not why I'm here."

Ethan kept his gaze off his watch and forced himself to wait patiently, wondering where this conversation was headed. He set the file on the desk to be recorded and leaned against the counter to take the weight off his leg.

"I suppose you've heard that Dr. Dixon is leaving our employ?"

Shock rocketed through him. Leaving? Already? "No, I hadn't heard." He wanted to ask the circumstances, but knew to speculate wouldn't leave a good impression.

"I'm sure I don't have to tell you what this means."

The shock faded and awareness dawned. Ethan straightened. No, he didn't need to be told. "What's the timeline?" *Don't sound so eager. Play it cool.*

"We need someone immediately. Dr. Dixon left with his things this morning."

Whoa. To say Dixon had given notice was one thing, but if he was *gone*—that meant Dixon had been fired. Doctors, especially the heads of departments, didn't leave like that unless forced. What had Dixon done?

Ethan hadn't liked the guy, held no respect for Dixon as a person, and as Jenn's cheating ex-husband, Dixon earned even more disgust from the family because of how he'd treated Jenn. Still, Ethan didn't wish anyone out of a job. "I see."

"The board is going to open the job to applicants once more and post the position as required. In the meantime we need an interim chief. We're also looking at other factors in our candidates, and considering how well-rounded our doctors are. Your service in Niger, for instance. We like knowing our doctors are compassionate to those in need. It looks good for the individual and for the hospital to have doctors willing to go into the field to perform humanitarian work."

So they'd been watching. He tried hard not to get too enthusiastic, not to let his thoughts run wild because he'd been disappointed once.

"Dr. Tulane, we'd like you to take on the role as interim chief until a final decision is made. It could take several months, but, of course, if you accept, weighted consideration will be given to your application."

A flash flood of satisfaction and pride surged through him. It was the job he'd worked toward since the start of his career, being handed to him on a silver platter. Finally.

"I'm sure you understand quite a few administrative duties are involved," Morrow continued. "The board thought it would give you more time to recover from your wound, but I see that's not needed. Your leg has healed?"

"Nearly one hundred percent, sir." His thigh throbbed in complaint.

"Good, good. Glad to hear it."

"Thank you." He smiled, unable to stop the grin forming on his lips. "I'm honored."

"But do you accept?" Mr. Morrow challenged, a twinkle in his eye. The man knew how badly Ethan wanted the position.

"I've been after the position for a long time, as I'm sure you know. Of course I accept."

Morrow dipped his head in acknowledgment and clapped one hand on Ethan's back, holding out his free hand to shake. "Then congratulations, Chief. I'll send out the notification this afternoon."

Ethan continued to smile as Morrow walked away, unable to believe the sudden change. Chief of surgery. It was the next step, the final step, to mark his career. The top of the ladder as he saw it. Some people in his position might want to move on to other, bigger hospitals, but not him. He wanted to be chief at this hospital, in his hometown.

He turned back to the desk to pick up the phone to call Jenn, and winced when his leg protested with a stab of pain. He needed to go relieve Jenn, needed to go do the therapy his physiotherapist had recommended. Needed to stay and get a feel for the new position he was about to take on. But what he really needed…was a plan on how to pull it all off.

MEGAN HAD GOTTEN UP earlier to shower and change, then returned to bed, her energy spent. Now she opened her eyes with a groan, aware that her body still ached in that flu type of way. But her chest didn't hurt as much, she actually felt stronger and she was hungry again. Why was it when you're sick all you want to do is eat and sleep?

A noise drew her attention. Simon was upset. His voice rose, high and shrill, and it sounded like it came from outside. But it was the tone responding to his upset that had Megan kicking the covers off her legs.

That wasn't Ethan. The voice was female, familiar. Jenn's.

Megan inhaled a steadying breath, and forced herself to a sitting position. The room wobbled as blood rushed to her head and she sat on the edge of the bed, coughing and hacking until the wooziness faded away.

On her feet, she finger-brushed her hair, got dressed and emerged from the bedroom wearing the freshly laundered jeans and sweatshirt she'd worn on the day of her arrival. Ethan or his housekeeper must have washed them for her.

Out in the main part of the house the living room was clear, the hall and Simon's bedroom, as well. Had she dreamed Jenn's voice? She'd had some pretty vivid dreams since being sick, memories of Sean and those awful nights, of sleeping in her car with those creeps knocking on her car windows and trying to buy sex.

Megan stopped just inside the swing door in the kitchen, her gaze fastening on Jenn and Simon outside in the backyard. Why wasn't her sister in school? Simon?

Jenn was trying to get Simon to color in a coloring book, but the kid stared morosely at the page, his head propped up on his palm in a way that made his cheek pull in a lopsided grimace. His cheeks were wet with tears and his shoulders shook with the force of his sobs. Oh, poor kid. He really was having a tough time of it.

Megan padded over toward the door only to pause. Simon was obviously safe and in good hands, but she needed an icebreaker with Jenn. No two ways about it.

The coffeepot beckoned and she blessed Ethan's taste in dark, thick, corrode-your-stomach brews. Megan hurriedly poured two cups and continued out the back door, aware of Jenn's panicked, leery expression when she looked up and saw Megan approaching. Hey, when opportunity knocked, you opened the door—and brought gifts. "I poured you a cup. Hey, Simon. What's the matter, bud?"

Jenn's mouth twitched. "No, thanks. I'm cutting back on caffeine."

Great. Jenn glared at her, Simon wouldn't look at her. *Feel the love.* Megan lifted a shoulder in a shrug. She wasn't a morning person, either. "That's okay. I usually have two cups. I'll drink it." Megan nudged Simon gently. "So, what's the problem? You're not having fun?" she asked in French.

"Leave him alone, Megan. Simon's had a difficult morning. Ethan dropped him off at preschool and he got so upset that he threw up and wouldn't stop screaming. The principal let me bring him home to stay until Ethan can get here from work. He'll be home any minute," she added, sounding a bit desperate. "We're fine if you want to go back inside and rest."

In other words, take a hike.

Megan took a sip of the coffee, her hands wrapped around the mug. Jenn stared at her, she stared at Jenn. Yeah, this was comfortable.

Should she blurt out what she had to say, or lead up to it? If Ethan was on his way home, time was running out and who knew when the next opportunity might arise where she had Jenn basically trapped and at her mercy? Her sister would never leave when she was responsible for Simon. "I'm sorry. Jenn—"

"Not now, Megs."

"But—"

"I said not now."

Whoa. Jenn had pulled out her teacher voice for that one. Megan seriously considered shutting up but stopped herself just in time. Screw it. She didn't have to listen to the teacher. She hadn't when she was in school, so why start now? "Look, I screwed up and I hurt you—"

"I have to get back to work as soon as Ethan returns and I don't want to be upset when I get there."

"Then don't get upset, just hear me out."

"No."

"When are you going to believe that I'm sorry, truly *sorry*, for what I did?"

Jenn nudged Simon to his feet, shooing him toward the bright and shiny new swing set. The boy turned, a crayon and his paper in his hands, and regarded them with a questioning stare. The tears had stopped but the stains were drying on his cheeks.

"Simon, go draw a picture or—or swing." Jenn moved her hand back and forth in an arc. "Go swing, Simon."

Simon glanced at her, and Megan jerked her head toward the slide, asking him to go play for a little bit so the grown-ups could talk.

Simon liked the slide. She'd watched from the kitchen table yesterday after dinner while he'd slid down over and over again.

"What did you say to him?" Jenn watched Simon carry his paper and crayon over to the structure. "The slide? Megan, I told him to swing. Ethan needs to get a guard for the top. It's too high. What if Simon falls?"

"Then he'll be smarter next time. Jenn, he's a kid. One who's come from Niger and has seen bullets and blood and death. The slide is a cakewalk." Once some things were experienced, there was no going back. "Everyone falls down. There's no guard against that."

Jenn looked insulted. "Ethan trusts me with Simon."

"And he still will. Simon played on the slide yesterday when Ethan was here and didn't fall once. He'll be fine. Stop being such a boring worrywart and listen to me."

Her baby sister stiffened, and Megan barely stopped herself from uttering a nasty curse. The taunting name had slipped out before she could stop it.

"Stop being such a worrywart and let me have some fun, will you?"

"But Mom said—"

"Get a life! Our parents are out of town and we have the house to ourselves. Hello? Teenagers are supposed to party, and that's exactly what I'm going to do. Pull the stick out of your butt and have some fun."

More memories came, things she'd said, things she wasn't proud of. Megan sighed and rubbed her head again. "What I meant was please, hear me out."

"That's not what you meant. I *know* what you meant. What you *always* meant."

She'd had to be a real bitch growing up, hadn't she? "That is the past. Jenn, I want to make this right. Can't you give me a chance to do that?"

Jenn shook her head back and forth. "No, because nothing you say *can* make it right. You can't undo what you did. And for the record? I'm not that pathetic schoolgirl anymore. You stay away from my husband or I'll kick your cheap, sorry butt all the way to the state line."

Megan felt her face heat with lava-like embarrassment. Then she smiled, admiring the backbone Jenn had finally developed. "Understood." Jenn blinked at Megan as though confused by her ready agreement. Like she was lying about that, too?

Her sister shoved her long hair behind her shoulder and harrumphed. "Did you ever once think that someone *had* to be a worrywart? That since that someone obviously wasn't *you*, because you couldn't be bothered even though you're older, it *had* to be me? Did you ever consider that maybe I got sick and tired of always *being* the responsible one?"

"Who said you had to be? No, really, you brought it up so let's talk about this and get everything out in the open," Megan said, following Jenn when she turned away and gathered up a plastic plate and juice box. "Who made you my keeper?"

Jenn's mouth opened and closed but no words came out. A frown formed and she busied herself with cleanup duty.

"Jenn...come on. Do you hate me because I didn't follow the rules, or because I did all the things you weren't brave enough to do?"

Chapter 9

JENN GASPED and swung around to face Megan. "Don't you *dare*."

"What if I did what I did because I wanted to escape all the crap at home? I never got to do anything that wasn't on that damn schedule."

Jenn inflated, puffing up like a blowfish. "Oh, you poor thing. To think that you had to go spend your days as the center of attention. You had *voice* lessons!"

"Which I hated. Just because a person can sing doesn't mean she wants to."

"Oh, and you hated gymnastics, too?"

"Like any girl wants dirty old men and perverted dads sitting there ogling them in skimpy little costumes talking about how *flexible* they are!"

"I couldn't get braces until I was in junior high but Dad bought you thousand-dollar gowns for those pageants."

"Where I got felt up by the judges and escorts because when I was twelve I looked like I was twenty."

Jenn tossed the items in her hands onto the table where

they landed with a clatter. "Don't. Don't stand there and feed me your latest lines of bull. You *liked* doing all that stuff. You reveled in it and rubbed it in my face every chance you got."

Megan had. She had because Jenn sucked at singing and wasn't coordinated and Megan was jealous that Jenn was allowed to stay home. While she'd cheered ball games, Jenn had snuggled up on the couch with Mom to read. While she'd played sports, Jenn had gone trick-or-treating and rode her bike. Jenn had been Mama's pet, allowed to stay home and spend her evenings cooking dinner and baking, laughing, visiting with Grandma. And Megan had looked down on Jenn because of it, hated her for it, even though she'd have given anything to be one of them and not an outsider.

Her father had made it worse, too. How many times had he told her not to worry about her schoolwork because, honestly, she wasn't that smart and her brains could only take her so far? According to Daddy Dearest, her looks were her best asset and she had to take advantage of them before she lost them. He'd belittled her abilities, destroyed her self-confidence. Made her unable to believe in herself for the longest time.

He wanted you dependent on him for your self-esteem, wanted to control you. You realize that now. You weren't Daddy's girl, you were Daddy's little alibi, and he took full advantage. Had Jenn ever figured out the truth of why their father was so gung-ho about taking Megan places? Once he'd dumped Megan off, the excuses had left him free to do—see—whomever he pleased. Could she really not know?

Megan shoved the pain aside. "I was a stupid kid and not very nice to you, but for the record," she said, her voice strengthening, "I have considered those things. I feel bad about them, too."

Jenn rolled her eyes. "Yeah, right."

"Don't give me that." Megan stepped toward her. "People change."

"Not you."

Her hands curled into fists. So she wasn't redeemable at all in Jenn's eyes? "Put yourself in my shoes. Have you ever thought about what it was like up on stage being picked apart by everyone watching? At any one time I was too fat for one judge and too skinny for another, my nose was too big, my thighs *jiggled* too much. I was *never* just right the way that I was, there was *always* something wrong with me." Years of trying, years of being talked to like she was a thing, *nothing*, washed over her. Years of knowing the truth about her father and being so ashamed of it she'd never talked to anyone about it—except once. *And you know how well that went.* Mama blamed her, not him. "I would've traded you, Jenn. I would've switched places with you in a heartbeat. Don't tell me I was the lucky one when you don't have a clue what it was like to stand there and be nothing."

The declaration seemed to throw Jenn off-kilter. But it was true. At first Megan had been happy to spend so much time with her dad. Jenn was little and always in her stuff and here was their handsome father showering Megan with attention and buying her beautiful things. She'd felt special. And their father was good. He knew the tricks, the lies, the ways to sidestep tough questions by taking his remarks to a personal level.

Whenever she'd asked where he disappeared to during her lessons or events, he'd criticized her. Her dance moves, her less-than-straight shoulders, the way she threw a ball or batted or landed a routine, like he'd actually stayed and watched. By the time he was through, she'd completely forgotten her question.

On a good day she was pretty and talented and his best girl, but on a bad one?

Only one news flash a day, Megs. You're treading water with Jenn the way it is. What does it matter now, anyway? This is about you and Jenn.

"None of this matters now," Jenn murmured, echoing Megan's thoughts. "None of it. You broke the bonds of trust when you slept with Sean. I'd always known you were capable of stuff like that with your so-called friends, but you did that to *me*, Megan, your *sister*. How would any woman trust her sister after that?"

"I'm not that girl anymore. I'm not, I swear it. Jenn, Sean wasn't a saint. He's not the man you've made him out to be all these years you've held this grudge. That night? I was trying to protect you. Everything I did was to try and keep you from making a huge mistake!"

"What mistake? Protect me from *what?*"

This was it, her chance to tell Jenn exactly what a low scum-sucking bottom-feeder Sean had been. But when Megan opened her mouth, words fled, just the way they had all those times someone had asked about the bruises and cuts and bloodied lips. She didn't want to admit that she'd hung around while someone beat the crap out of her. Who would? But if she didn't say it now, didn't connect with Jenn now, when? "He hit me."

The voice didn't sound like hers. It was low and soft and full of shame and she hated, *hated*, that Jenn now knew one of her dirty, shameful secrets. But it was too late to take it back or blow it off because Jenn had heard her. She could tell by the way Jenn froze in place, the way her eyes flared wide.

Megan's pride kicked in as always. "You always said you hoped I got everything I deserved for stealing Sean from you. Well, rest assured Sean made sure I got more than that." She laughed, trying for light and breezy but ending up with strained and forced. "I mean, you know how he got when he drank, loud and obnoxious, any little thing would tick him off. After a while, the thing that ticked him off most was the sight of me."

Jenn couldn't have looked more shocked—or suspicious. "If this is another one of your stories, Megan, so help me—Is that true?"

If? A story? Getting beat up wasn't something to joke about, not even for Megan.

"Why didn't you say anything? Tell us?"

A bitter laugh welled in her throat. "Who would I have told? You don't believe me now." Another caustic laugh erupted from within her. Of course this was how things would go, eh? "Mom and Dad kicked me out. You hadn't spoken to me since that night. I was pregnant, and the way I looked at it, I didn't have a lot of options. You were right about one thing, though. I was spoiled and self-centered and shallow, because in the beginning I honestly thought Sean's money could make up for being slapped around."

Jenn's expression was priceless as she sorted through what Megan had said. If only she had a camera.

Jenn lifted her hands and pressed them to her head, her face scrunched up like a kid about to take medicine. "I can't…I can't think."

What was there to think about? Either Jenn believed it or she didn't. Either she let Megan stay, or she didn't.

"I can't believe you didn't tell us."

Honesty came easier here. "Sean was good. A day didn't go by that I didn't hear him say something about how I'd betrayed all of you, how much you hated me, wouldn't care what happened to me. You get told something so much and after a while you believe it."

An engine cut from somewhere in the neighborhood and a door slammed, the sound echoing off the trees.

"I'm sorry," Jenn said softly. "I am, truly. I had no idea, and I'm very, very sorry you had to deal with that after you married Sean. But," she stressed, her tone firming, "what Sean did during your marriage is irrelevant to what happened between us and what led up to your marriage. It doesn't change how you treated me or what you did." Jenn gathered up the crayons with an angry scoop of her hand and pushed them into the box with little jabs of her finger. "And even though people change, I still know there's another reason that you're here. What do you want, Megan? It can't simply be the need for forgiveness."

"Why can't it?"

"Because I gave you tons of chances growing up. I forgave you when you broke the porcelain doll Dad got me when you went away for that sectionals meet. I forgave you when all the recipes I copied from Grandma's box wound up getting thrown out in the trash or when you *lost* the autographed copy of Nancy Drew Mom gave me for Christmas. I forgave you each and every time I had to cast my vote for whatever stupid school contest you were in, and every single time you turned around and stabbed me in the back when I wasn't looking."

Jenn's words were so painfully telling. Megan had done those things, uncaring of Jenn's feelings because she'd known Jenn would forgive her eventually, striking out because she could. Because she'd felt she had to. Strike out, or implode.

But she didn't want to be thought of as that shallow, selfish girl anymore. Didn't want to be the sister Jenn couldn't count on, was embarrassed of, ashamed of, hated.

She'd made a mistake, *lots* of mistakes. Couldn't Jenn see that things hadn't been perfect? She had to stop pretending that their childhood was a fairy tale. Dad's comments had hurt Jenn, too.

"But why bother asking for my forgiveness now?"

Because Sean had promised her she would see him again, that she'd never get away. He'd promised her that she'd pay for what she'd done and she knew he'd keep his word. "Because I want to start fresh. Can't we put the past behind us and act like sisters? The way sisters are supposed to act? Can't we try?"

Jenn stared at her, every emotion crossing her face— disbelief, pain, derision, guilt. "Maybe. If I could trust you. But I can't. You say you've changed but *how* do I know it's true? Megan, sisters aren't supposed to sleep with their sister's boyfriends! Considering you've done that to me *twice*…why would I believe you?"

"It was one time. *Once.*"

"She slept with your boyfriend? That's what all the drama is about?" Ethan emerged from the house and walked toward them, his gaze searching Megan's as though concerned.

Megan's heart thumped in her chest. He looked sexy and confident and way too appealing to a girl who'd sworn off men. And now he knew—not that it was much of a secret. He could have asked Nick or Jenn at any time and they probably would've told him.

But what all had he heard? Her cheeks flushed with shame. Ethan would have to arrive that moment, wouldn't he?

"Megan doesn't respect boundaries," Jenn said softly, her voice thick with tears. "If she sees a guy she wants, nothing stops her."

Her gorgeous host didn't comment, but Megan caught the nearly imperceptible wince he performed at the news. Because he thought she was easy?

She wanted the ground to swallow her. She wasn't a slut. The first time Jenn had "lost a boyfriend" wasn't her fault. Bryan What's-His-Name had broken up with Jenn, claiming he was in love with Megan instead, just because he'd been hanging out at the house a lot. *Hello*, not her problem. She hadn't given him any encouragement.

But Sean…She had to accept blame for that—up to a point.

"So you're mad at her for taking a boyfriend, even though you're now happily married to Nick? So that's why he's been in such a mood."

Jenn's cheeks turned a bright, bright red. "It's the fact that she did it, Ethan, that she hurt me that way. Not that I regret that it happened."

"Well—" he lifted a hand and rubbed the back of his neck, a contemplative frown on his gorgeous face "—if you don't regret that it happened, what's all the fuss about?"

ETHAN FOUGHT his frustration with the sisters and tried to remember that in the heat of the moment, forgiveness was hard to give. So he chose to play dumb and focus on the obvious. "Something to think about, eh?"

He managed a smile and tried to calm the situation with a change in topic. Simon was nearby and who knew how long the girls had been at it with him listening? "Jenn, thanks again for bringing Simon home."

Simon sat atop the slide, hard at work on something.

Jenn finished poking the crayons in the box. "I'm glad they caught him before he made it off school grounds."

Megan inhaled and cast a worried glance over to where Simon sat. "Wait a minute. You said he got upset and sick. He tried to run away again?"

Boyfriend stealer or not, Megan had a compassionate heart. Ethan liked that she'd come to care for Simon so quickly. "A last-minute spot opened up at the preschool located in the elementary school where Jenn works, but Simon didn't appreciate the effort it took to get it for him. I was in surgery, so the principal called Jenn when he couldn't get Simon calmed down."

"I was glad to help."

Ethan smirked. Jenn was polite as always even though he knew good and well she would've rather swum with sharks than spend the morning with Megan.

"Simon's probably getting hungry and tired. We've been outside since we got here."

No doubt to avoid waking Megan. "I ran through a drive-through. You're welcome to join us. I bought plenty."

"No, but thanks." Jenn glanced at Megan, then quickly away again. "I need to get going."

He watched Megan for a clue as to whether or not he needed to press Jenn to stay.

Jenn pasted on a smile but it didn't reach her eyes. "Ethan, I hate to say it but I think keeping Simon in private day care or maybe hiring someone one-on-one until he adjusts is probably your best bet."

"Any recommendations?"

"You're getting a late start on the school year. Day care is always a problem in this town. There just aren't enough approved providers." Jenn fingered her watch, looking anxious as she glanced down at the time. "I'll check with the other teachers and get back to you. Simon isn't ready and he needs to become acclimated in stages. You've signed him up for classes, right?"

"Yeah. Most of them start next week."

"That's perfect."

"Except that I have to find care for him while I'm at work."

Jenn quickly straightened the coloring books and crayons, putting everything on the outdoor table in neat little stacks. Every now and again she glanced at Megan, studying her as though trying to figure out what to believe.

"Leave those. I'll put them aw—" Ethan broke off, staring just past Megan's hip as Simon approached them with his head down, feet dragging.

"Hey, Simon. What do you have there?" Megan asked in French.

Simon pulled his other hand from behind his back and shyly showed her the crumpled piece of paper he carried. Apparently he'd sat at the top of the structure and drawn a picture—that's what he'd been working on so intently.

Megan set the coffee mug on the table and accepted the gift with a smile. "*Merci*. Thank you, Simon."

Ethan moved close until he could see it. Simon had drawn stick figures of varying height and color. But there was no mistaking the woman in the drawing. The picture was of Megan, Simon and himself. She and Simon stood hand in hand while he…What the hell?

In the picture he carried a doctor bag with the Doctors Without Borders emblem on it. He stood separate from her and Simon, a frown on his face and looking quite fierce, by a box? The little box had a circle on top with smoke coming off it.

"It's beautiful, Simon. Good job."

Ethan reached out to take the picture so he could get a closer look. Megan released it to give Simon a hug, and he studied the drawing with a frown much like the one in the picture. Finally the lightbulb came on and he felt a surge of wry embarrassment. The stove.

Niger had sent him back to the States with a new

penchant for overcooking everything, just so he knew it wasn't raw or half-done as the food had been there. He made a mental note to back off on the heat.

"Great picture, Simon." Jenn straightened. "Ethan, I hate to be rude, but I have to get back to school. My lesson plans have to be turned in before tomorrow's in-school service meeting."

Ethan's attention shifted to Jenn. "I thought the principal said there wasn't any school?"

"For the kids. Teachers have to report, though."

The timing of it couldn't have been worse. "There's no way you can watch Simon tomorrow?"

"No, I won't be available again until Saturday. Sorry. Maybe Nick could take him to the garage and watch him?"

"I don't want Simon around all that traffic."

"Good point."

"I hate to ask but could you take a personal day?"

"No. School policy is that we can't use any of them until a couple months into the year. Exceptions are sometimes given but I don't think your babysitting woes would qualify as an emergency."

Ethan rubbed the back of his neck in a sad attempt to ease the tension before he twisted and turned his head, sighing when it popped loudly. "I have a 6:00 a.m. surgery tomorrow morning followed by meetings all day." Another smile formed and he didn't try to hold it back. "I've, uh, been appointed interim chief of surgery."

Jenn's mouth dropped. "What? What happened to Todd being Chief?"

"Todd, who? Your ex-husband, Todd?" Megan asked, confused.

Ethan nodded. "Dixon was appointed chief several months ago. And I don't know what happened, but he isn't chief now. One of the board directors asked me to fill in until a final decision is made."

Jenn smiled her first sincere smile since he'd arrived to find her and Megan in a huddle.

"Oh, Ethan, congratulations!"

He held up his hands. "It's not a done deal. And after last time I know better than to count on getting it. I'm just playing it by ear. In the meantime, I'll have to contact the hospital day care and see if they'll give Simon one more shot."

Simon began jerking on Megan's hand. "No, no! No day care, no day care."

Ethan scowled and lowered himself to Simon's level, grasping the boy's shoulder to gain eye contact. How sad was it that those were Simon's first real words in English? "Simon, stop. Simon? We don't have a choice. You're going to day care."

MEGAN CRINGED at Ethan's lousy French—and the way the kid backed away from Ethan when he knelt to speak to Simon. In Ethan's defense, she knew he'd been nothing but gentle and caring when taking care of Simon —she'd watched them interact enough now to know that. But Simon still removed himself from Ethan's grasp and backed away until he was behind her legs, staring up at Megan as though he expected her to make everything better.

Yeah, right, kid. I can't fix my own problems.

"Maybe your mother or Gram can watch him?" Jenn suggested.

Megan listened, more than a little upset herself. In between naps, she'd gotten to know Simon better. He was quiet, too shy, and had to be drawn into conversation. He wouldn't make friends easily, not at this stage and especially not with a language barrier.

"Gram's got that virus that's going around, and Mom's working overtime on some big real estate deal. They're not available."

Simon hugged her legs, big tears swimming in his beautiful eyes. "Tu peu me garder S'il-te plaît, Mademoiselle Megan. Je serai gentil."

"What did he say?"

Megan felt Simon trembling, saw the fear and upset in his eyes and knew she couldn't say no. "He, um…He wants me to watch him."

Chapter 10

ETHAN NARROWED HIS GAZE in contemplation while Jenn's head swung back and forth like a rag doll in a two-year-old's hands.

"He did not say that. Megan, you're making that up."

"Actually, he did," Ethan drawled.

Jenn laughed, the sound strained. "No, that's a horrible idea. Ethan, seriously."

"Are you feeling up to it?"

"If she's feeling that good, then she needs to be *on her way.*" Jenn gave Megan a death glare. "What about that job you mentioned?"

Megan had Ethan's undivided attention, and she felt her cheeks heat, which was hysterical since she had considered the ability to blush a lost art after all she'd experienced. "I've, um, felt better. And the job is sort of up in the air."

"I knew it," Jenn murmured.

"Look, the point is you can't take Simon back to a place that obviously can't keep track of him."

"Megan, don't do this. Caring for a child is a big responsibility."

"Yes, it is," Ethan murmured, "but Megan already has a bond with Simon and she isn't well enough to travel yet. I could use the help."

Megan was thankful for the support, backhanded though it was. "And people change," she felt compelled to add. "Jenn, I'm not a teenager anymore. I can certainly handle coloring books and games for a few days. It's not my normal thing, I'll admit, but we'd be fine long enough for you to find a day-care solution Simon can handle."

"No day care!"

Never taking her eyes off Ethan and ignoring Jenn entirely, Megan gave Simon's arm a reassuring pat.

The tension in Ethan's face eased a bit. "If you're sure you're up for it, it sounds like a great idea. You understand him, which is more than most people here can do."

Jenn's arms flopped to her sides and she glared at Megan. It was a good thing Jenn looked good with some color in her cheeks, because with Megan around Jenn always seemed to be sporting it.

"It's the least I can do after you've taken me in and cared for me." Megan couldn't resist that little dig. If Jenn had let her stay at her house, she wouldn't be indebted to Ethan now would she? "Maybe I can help Simon with his English. I'm not a teacher but I can work with him on the basics."

Ethan rubbed his hands together and practically melted at her feet with relief, the tension draining from his shoulders. "That would be fantastic. It's settled, then. Megan will be Simon's temporary nanny until she's rested and recovered and I find a qualified alternative."

Megan refused to let Jenn's you've-got-to-be-kidding-me stare make her feel guilty. She could do this. Simon was a kid. She might not be a rocket scientist, but she and Simon could pull this off. They were tight. He wouldn't run away from her.

You hope.

"It's a paying position. I insist."

Ethan held up a hand as though to stall her protest, not that she was going to protest cash. It sorta made the world go round and when you didn't have it, the world kept on going while you came to a screeching halt. She would've liked to protest, to counter the offer with something that would have wiped Jenn's superior, *here we go* expression right off her face, but she wasn't a fool. Cash was good, the more, the sooner, the better.

"I'd have to pay for child care elsewhere, and if you can help him with the things he needs to learn, you'll more than earn the pay."

"Thanks, I appreciate it. I feel bad, though, since I've already taken advantage of you." The double entendre didn't hit her until after the words left her mouth.

Jenn gaped and turned beet-red, and Ethan just stood there, his weight balanced on his uninjured leg, a lazy smile pulling at his lips.

Megan sighed. Open mouth, insert foot. She hadn't said it on purpose but the look on Jenn's face stated loud and clear that Jenn thought Megan had already tangled some sheets with Ethan or else it wouldn't be long before she did.

Megan gritted her teeth. The more she thought about it, the more she realized she was safer here than any other destination she might have in mind. Beauty was perfect. Her trip to see Jenn was supposed to have been temporary and last only long enough for her to get well and make amends. But why not stay for a while? If Sean was out there looking for her, this was the last place he'd ever think to search, and he'd be way off her trail by the time she packed up and left.

She could keep a low profile, earn some cash and maybe while she was there, she could talk to Jenn and bring her around. If time and physical presence didn't work, fine, but no one could say she hadn't tried.

"I wish," Ethan teased, earning yet another glare from Jenn.

The comment pulled at Megan's heartstrings, though, because Ethan followed it with a conspiratorial wink of support. He wasn't falling for Jenn's warnings of doom and gloom. The wink and statement might have freaked her out before but not now. It was light, flirtatious, not a heavy-duty come on. And it helped that not once during their time together had Ethan behaved as anything other than a gentleman. But Jenn didn't need to know the flirting meant nothing, did she?

"So you'll do it?"

Megan smiled down at Simon's upturned face. "I'd love to."

"Oh, Ethan." Jenn grabbed her purse from the table and gripped it like a grandma in a neighborhood of hoodlums. "You are so going to regret this."

AFTER JENN LEFT, Megan returned to the house to get plates and drinks for the lunch Ethan had left on the countertop. Ethan figured she needed some time alone after her run-in with her sister.

Ethan shook his head. Megan had slept with Jenn's boyfriend? Married him?

He was the last one who could throw stones when it came to sexual adventures, but even he knew better than to mess around with one of his brothers' girlfriends, former or otherwise. People said time could heal wounds, and all the Tulanes knew that well after the falling-out with Nick years back.

Ethan had done the right thing by asking Megan to stick around. She wasn't a bad person—kids didn't respond to bad people the way Simon responded to Megan—but she'd apparently made some poor choices. Who hadn't?

Ethan watched Simon play, wondering if this was one of his. Not that he regretted adopting Simon—not for a moment. But had returning to Beauty and forcing Simon to adapt been a wise decision? Would he ever get to a point where he was comfortable with the boy? Simon was a good kid and except for the day-care dilemma, Ethan barely knew the boy was around. But that was part of the problem. He and Simon couldn't seem to connect. He didn't know what Simon wanted from him, and he felt like a total screwup because he didn't know what to do.

Simon never said he was hungry, never spoke up and said he had to go to the bathroom, nothing. The only time the boy talked was if he was asked a direct question and pressed for an answer.

So unless Ethan remembered to periodically feed Simon and nudge the boy toward the toilet…

Simon climbed the slide for the tenth time and Ethan watched as the boy who'd clung to him to keep from being left in day care now wanted nothing to do with him. Which was why the relief he'd felt when Megan said she'd stay on and help with Simon had practically given him a head rush it was so potent.

How did Garret and Nick do this? Garret had Darcy to help take care of their infant daughter, but Nick had raised Matt on his own for eight years until meeting Jenn, and he'd been estranged from the family then, too. How had Nick figured out what to do?

Simon rarely made eye contact, and had never talked to anyone other than Ethan except to scream at Jenn and the day-care workers that he wanted to go home.

Except for Megan. He talks to her and obviously likes her. This'll work.

But for how long? How long would Megan stay?

How long would it take for her to recover? Would Jenn come around and forgive her sister before Megan got tired of saying she was sorry and took off?

The past couple days of waiting on Megan, caring for her and hearing her cry out in her sleep…Nick was right. There was more to Megan's story. People didn't say those things, make those sounds in their sleep, unless something bad had happened to them.

Like Simon.

Ethan frowned, noticing that every few seconds the boy looked toward the door as though searching for Megan. Ethan couldn't blame him. Megan was pretty, understood French and had a wicked sense of humor Simon had probably picked up on. They were two of a kind in a wounded kind of way. Maybe they could help each other somehow and in the process, help him figure out how to heal them.

Not a problem—unless she's as irresponsible as Jenn says. What'll you do then?

A knot formed in his gut at the thought. Was he making a mistake? Surely Jenn was exaggerating? Convenience was one thing, but he couldn't put Simon's safety at risk.

"Simon?" Ethan waited, noting that Simon stilled but didn't raise his gaze from the rocks he played with. Twelve hundred dollars in play equipment and repairs to the tree house at the edge of the woods and the kid played with rocks. It just proved how off track he was in his parental thinking. "It's time for lunch. Food," he said in halting French, then English, emphasizing the English words as the pediatrician had said to do. "Let's go inside."

Head down, Simon ignored him.

"Simon, it's time to eat now. Let's go."

Simon carefully stacked his pile of rocks, his shoulders hanging low. The boy probably didn't understand why he'd been pulled from his homeland, flown halfway around the world. But maybe in time he could help Simon forget what had happened in Niger.

How do you forget your uncle getting gunned down and dying in front of you in a bloody heap?

Ethan made his way to the back door, his shoulders low much like the boy's in front of him.

Isa, my friend, what were you thinking? What if I'm not ready to be a father?

THE REST OF THE WEEK passed in a fog of lazing on the couch and coloring pictures with Simon, watching Disney movies and fixing easy snacks and meals. Doing so took all the energy Megan managed to muster, but by week's end she finally began to feel like her old self. Her energy was coming back, she wasn't coughing nearly as much and she'd put on a few of the pounds she'd lost since Sean's release from prison.

Megan had even gotten the courage to leave a message on Jenn's machine, asking her to come over, to call, to talk, but Jenn had yet to respond.

Did you really think she would?

Megan had been in town almost two weeks. Wasn't it time?

The wood trim of the door frame bit into Megan's shoulder and she shifted to relieve the ache, watching as Ethan tucked the sheet and blanket around Simon's waist. She felt a tug in her heart even though she warned herself against it.

Temporary gig, Megs. No bonding allowed.

"Good night, Simon."

Ethan's broad hand smoothed gently over Simon's closely cropped hair. The image was sweet. Tender. Unbelievably sexy.

You're not interested.

True. But she'd never thought she could love a job so much, temporary or not. There was something so satisfying about caring for the little boy, being the one he depended on. Ethan had worked late all week, transitioning into his new role at the hospital. But when he got home, evenings were filled with Simon's bath, lots of bedtime stories then getting Simon settled for the night.

Yeah, what about those nights?

She focused on Ethan's dark hair, the play of muscles beneath his shirt, images filling her head. She was drawn to him physically, even though there was a constant monologue in her head warning her away.

The thing about living with someone was that two weeks was plenty of time to get to know her host a little better. Alone in the house with Simon in bed, she and Ethan had made small talk at first, discussed the weather, the upcoming winter Tennessee was supposed to have. All the inane things strangers discussed when it seemed as though they were both distracted by thoughts of other things.

Like what he looks like nekkid?

She inhaled and struggled to focus. What amazed her was how down-to-earth Ethan was. The stories he told about the scrapes and stunts he and his brothers had pulled as kids…They were funny and sweet and ornery and they made her laugh until her sides hurt. She shared stories of her and Jenn, too, focusing on the few good times she remembered rather than the bad. Slim pickings those were.

When she couldn't keep her eyes open a moment longer she'd collapse into bed in an exhausted stupor, then Ethan would open up the mound of paperwork he carted home and work even more hours.

How he managed to stay awake was beyond her. She was brain-dead by 9:00 p.m., quite a change from her night-owl tendencies created by waiting tables until one and two o'clock.

"Megan? Simon said good-night."

Megan blinked to awareness at the sound of Ethan's voice and shoved herself off the doorjamb. She smiled as she approached the stained wooden bed covered in a brown, blue and cream blanket. The walls of Simon's room matched the blue in the coverlet and there were beautiful framed pictures of horses on the wall, creating a Western theme without being too little-kid cutesy. "You have good dreams tonight, okay, sugar?"

That was something she had in common with the boy. Twice now she'd woken up in the wee hours of the morning after a nightmare only to discover Simon huddled and asleep in a corner in her room. She'd carry him back to bed and tuck him in, and in the dark they'd whisper and talk about ice cream and slides and strawberry preserves.

Megan settled herself on the bed and leaned over Simon's too-thin form to give him a kiss and hug. Unlike the boy's standoffish behavior with Ethan, he curled his arms around her neck and squeezed and whispered for her to stay. Her eyes stung.

Man, maybe the saying was true. Maybe everyone did

need a certain number of hugs a day. In the last week she'd grown to count on Simon's embraces because they made her feel so good.

"Mangeons-nous de la crème glacé demain?"

She winked at him. "I'd love to."

"Est-ce que tu es encore malade?"

"No, sweetie." She saw the worry in his face and hated that she'd put it there with all her coughing and lying about. "I'm feeling much better now. The medicine Dr. Ethan gave me helped. I'm almost good as new."

"Peux-tu me raconté un autre histoire?"

Ah, so that's what he wanted.

"Not now, Simon. No more stories tonight, it's late." Ethan's deep voice held a wealth of authority, brooking no argument.

"Time for sleep," she added, gentling her tone when Simon gave Ethan a wary glance. "I'll read to you tomorrow."

Simon shot Ethan another look but nodded his understanding and rolled to his side, crossing his arms one over the other in front of him, knees drawn to his chest in a defensive pose.

Oh, baby boy. How many times had she fallen asleep that way, hoping to defend herself from the bogeyman who always came in the dark of night? Listening to her parents fight and curse each other in hoarse whispers. Listening for the sound of Sean's footsteps after a night of boozing it up.

Megan got to her feet to follow Ethan from the room, but on the path to the door she paused, unable to leave Simon so alone. She remembered that feeling, that knot in her stomach making her sick, huddling beneath the blankets afraid to breathe, afraid to draw attention. Just... afraid. She couldn't leave Simon that way.

A dark brown bookcase towered in the corner like a

soldier on guard, its floor-to-ceiling shelves holding books, older, obviously used kiddie-games she'd learned used to belong to Ethan's nephew, Matt.

Megan spied something dark that nearly blended into the woodwork, a stuffed animal that had been tucked into one of the higher shelves where Simon couldn't reach it. The sight reminded her of the movie they'd watched that afternoon. Woody had been shelved, as well, the worst, most disastrous thing that could happen to a toy.

The stuffed animal turned out to be a dog. Not a new toy from the looks of it, but it was soft and in good shape with big, floppy ears only slightly worn, a black thread snout and happy little eyes.

She carried the dog to the bed, holding its ear to her mouth as though talking to it while she petted it and shared secret words. Simon was instantly intrigued.

"Have you met Simon? He lives here, too. Simon, have you met—What? Oh, you poor thing! You don't have a name?" She clucked and fussed and used her fingers to make the dog's head lower as though very sad. "Poor doggie. Well, don't feel too bad. I know Simon would be happy to meet you and give you a name, wouldn't you?" she asked softly in French, not repeating the words in English because it was late and they were both tired.

Simon didn't move, didn't respond except to follow the animal and whatever movement she made it do. Megan playfully walked the dog up Simon's side to his chest then nuzzled the dog's nose in Simon's neck.

The little boy hesitantly reached out and curled his fingers in the animal's fluffy coat.

"There, see? Now you both have a friend and no one has to be afraid. Maybe you can give him a name, too, eh, Simon? You'll let him sleep with you, right? So he won't be scared and sad sitting up there on the shelf by himself?"

Simon nodded and when he did, Megan made the dog's head shift and she made a smooching sound. All the playacting paid off when Simon finally smiled, his big mocha eyes looking so relieved the lump reappeared in her throat.

"It'll all be okay, sugar. You'll see." She smoothed her fingers over Simon's cheek and felt the child's trembling. So scared. So small. Her heart broke. "It'll be okay," she whispered again, slowly beginning to sing the only French lullaby she knew. The trembling stopped and Simon's lashes slowly lowered and stayed shut, but she kept singing, wishing she could take all his fear away.

When her back ached from leaning over him so long, she straightened. "Sweet dreams, sugar." She leaned over and bussed a kiss on his forehead, breathing in the scent of soap and boy and fabric softener.

Head down, heart aching, Megan was almost to the door before she looked up and realized Ethan had returned and stood outside in the hall watching them.

Acutely aware of his gaze and not quite comfortable because of it, she turned off the light and pulled Simon's door mostly closed, remembering how as a girl she'd liked having the door open just a tad.

She flashed Ethan a self-conscious smile, embarrassed. If Sean had seen what she'd done he would have laughed at her, told her how stupid she was for giving in to Simon, for playacting with the stuffed toy, for being soft.

"If you're not too tired, I'd like to talk to you before you go to bed. There's something I want to discuss in regard to Simon."

Oh, that sounded ominous.

It was a long walk down the short hallway, each step bringing with it a memory. Sean's instructions and lectures on how she should behave, what she'd done wrong. Was whatever Ethan wanted to discuss in the same vein?

Maybe the dog was an antique and Ethan didn't want Simon playing with it? She should have asked before handing over the toy. But why put it in Simon's room if it wasn't to be played with?

Her steps slowed even more, her thoughts jumbled. What if Ethan had found a new day-care provider? The time had flown by, but how could she not have realized? He'd had plenty of time to contact a center or hire an individual babysitter. Had he? So soon?

That was it. It had to be. He'd found someone and was going to break the news to her. But with only a week's pay and no contact from Jenn, where did that leave Megan? She wanted to stay here, *needed* to stay here so Sean wouldn't find her. Wanted to be Simon's nanny and see him grow, at least help him adjust. Temporary or not, she needed that little boy as much as he needed her.

"Let's go outside on the deck."

She nodded once, slowly, her footsteps dragging along with death-row precision. With no contact and certainly no sympathy from Jenn, she was homeless again.

Chapter 11

ETHAN WATCHED as Megan swallowed. Her fingers curled into tight little fists and she squared her shoulders, like she had when she'd faced Jenn. What was up with that? She looked like she was facing a firing squad.

He grabbed a throw off the couch and carried it with him, nodding when she murmured she was going to get a drink and would join him in a moment. He'd built a small fire in the pit earlier in the evening, the mesh grate in place over top of it to keep any small ash from floating up in the breeze and flying into the woods surrounding the house.

A few minutes passed, but Ethan didn't mind waiting. It gave him some time to clear his head of the stress and problems of the day, and to go over his plan one more time. Was he making the right choice?

It was no wonder parents were frazzled all the time. The daily decisions were overwhelming.

The door opened and closed behind him, and without a word he indicated the seat positioned next to his. Megan left a mug of tea on the arm of his chair as she settled herself. He handed her the throw and caught the small look of surprise that he'd considered her comfort. Her ex-husband must have really been a class-A jerk.

"This is nice."

"Yeah." He lifted the mug. "Thanks."

"It's supposed to help you relax. I found it in the cupboard."

A gift from Alex. His baby sister was always buying them gifts she thought they needed. Dress shoes for Luke because he was prone to wear sneakers with his suits. Manly-smelling essential oils for Garret so that when Darcy gave Garret a massage he didn't come away smelling like a flower. For him it was tea. Alex had bought the stuff after crashing at his place for Nick's wedding because their parents' house was full to the brim with out-of-town relatives, and she'd gotten tired of finding him up roaming around. But right now, a good stiff drink might serve him better, especially since his plan had to include keeping his hands off Megan in order for it to work. "I owe you an apology."

Megan turned her face away and looked out at the darkness around them, inhaling deeply and closing her eyes. The light from the fire flickered over her profile, high-lighting the soft curves and smooth planes and lips he'd noticed far too frequently lately and ached to taste. Just once. But who was he kidding? Once wouldn't be enough, not with a woman like her.

"Why?"

Ethan smiled at her bluntness. Any other woman would've acted surprised and said he didn't owe her anything, or simply responded with a polite, "Oh?" But not Megan. They were strangers cohabiting, and yet she was blunt and bold and he liked it that she didn't walk on eggshells around him. So many women played games, said one thing but meant another, like guys were supposed to be able to read their minds. He liked Megan's plainspoken honesty, though he was well aware of Jenn's beliefs to the contrary.

"I know you were hoping to get a chance to talk to Jenn, but with her working all day and me not getting home until later in the evening, you've been too exhausted to go see her." He didn't think it possible but Megan tensed even more in her seat.

"That's okay. No, really, it is. I've tried, you know? I apologized and did my best to make up, but it's up to her if she calls me back. And frankly even if she did call, we'd probably wind up back at square one. We, uh, tend to do that."

He mulled that over, deciding to be as blunt. He hadn't mentioned Jenn's accusation, but maybe it was time to get it all out in the open before he broached the subject he wanted to talk to her about. "Most girls know not to sleep with their sister's boyfriend."

Her head lowered, her expression sardonic. "Yeah, well, sometimes things happen that you don't expect."

Things like what? Something inside him reared in anger, his suspicions running wild. Sean was the name Megan had cried out in her fever-ridden sleep. The rest of the sounds and noises she'd made had been mostly incoherent, but he'd recognized the name. The fear.

"Sean, don't. Please, don't. No."

Last night when she'd cried out in her dreams it had been everything he could do not to go into her room and hold her…comfort her, and not like the way she'd just comforted Simon in his bedroom. "So…Sean was the boyfriend? Your husband?"

"*Ex*-husband. Yeah. Look, Ethan, if you have something to say, just say it. Don't beat around the bush, okay?"

Ethan scowled at the fire, not letting her push him into

saying something he shouldn't. He wanted to know more about what Sean had done to her and why she'd had to beg, but the topic wasn't any of his business and a part of him—the one so freshly home from Niger—wasn't ready to hear another tragic, unthinkable story about a woman being abused.

Ethan sipped the tea to take his focus off his turbulent thoughts, wincing at the taste. He hadn't liked it when Alex brewed it for him, either.

"So," she said softly when he didn't speak. "Are you sitting there trying to think of a nice way to ask me to leave?"

He glanced at her in amusement. "Quite the opposite. Megan, I need to know if you're sincere about making up with Jenn."

She released a rough huff of a laugh. "What's she said now?"

"Nothing. I'm asking because families protect their own and as a Tulane, Jenn's one of us. But if you're sincere…"

"What? You'll help me convince her to give me a chance?"

"Yeah, I will."

The light from the fire shadowed half of her face when she turned toward him, clearly befuddled. "Why?"

That wasn't as easy to answer. "Because I know what it's like to make a wrong move and regret it. I also know how easy it is to fight with a sibling and have things get blown out of proportion because everyone involved is too close to the moment."

Ethan turned his attention to the flames, his thoughts barreling back to a time when Nick was so estranged from the family he'd cross the street to avoid them. Being the oldest and a college freshman majoring in pre-med, Ethan had felt superior to his younger, obviously idiotic sibling, and he'd run his mouth way more than he should, ordering Nick around, spouting off. Something he'd always regretted. "As to how I'll do it…I've been thinking. I've made a few inquiries into day care and the more I hear and see, the more I appreciate the progress you've made with Simon. You said the job in Chicago wasn't guaranteed. So why not stay here and be Simon's full-time, live-in nanny?"

He thought she'd be happy, relieved. At least show a favorable response. Instead she looked at him with blatant suspicion, her features carefully banked. A spark of life shone through, as if she liked the idea, but was leery.

"What's the catch?"

He didn't like the hesitation in her tone, like he was going to demand sex and she was waiting for the snarky proposal. Sex and babysitting for a roof over her head. Some guys would do it. And maybe, before Niger, he would've suggested it, too. But like Megan had told Jenn last week, people change. Including him. He hadn't exactly been a choirboy, but he wouldn't take advantage of Megan's situation. "No catch. I need someone I can trust with my son, and you have reasons for wanting to be here, which means you'll do your best to keep your job. In the past week, you've proven your patience and kindness with Simon, and I figured we could help each other out."

Megan rose and walked to the railing where the firelight didn't reach. A cool breeze blew, bringing with it a combination of her perfume and something uniquely Megan. Watching her, he noticed the slenderness of her body, the delicate way the firelight played over her form.

Those long hours at work are going to come in handy.

Because even though Megan drew his interest sexually, he'd do whatever it took to keep Simon laughing, including ignoring his baser needs and his attraction to his beautiful houseguest.

In the time she'd been here Megan had changed the balance of things. Now he was able to see what was missing, what Simon responded to and liked.

Reminded of the scene in Simon's bedroom, a pained grimace pulled at his lips. "Do you know Simon's been here five weeks now and I never once thought to give him something to sleep with?"

She stared out at the night, her shoulders lowering a little at the praise. "You've had a lot on your mind."

He set the tea aside and joined her at the railing, leaning against the banister and gazing up at the blanket of darkness highlighted by the moon's glow. The air was crisp and cool, a perfect fall night—for a confession? "Megan, I'm out of my element and over my head." Ethan lowered his elbows to the rail and clasped his hands together, staring off at the tree house at the edge of the yard.

He glanced at Megan and found her staring at him, watchful, listening. And the urge to kiss her was so powerful he had to look away and force himself to continue. "I planned on coming home from Niger with a fresh perspective, not a child. I figured…I hoped to have a family one day but I was going to do it in order. Marriage, honeymoon, kids. I didn't plan on having this responsibility until I'd reached a point in my life when I thought I was ready. You'll probably think it's a guy thing, but when I made that promise to Isa, I thought it wouldn't be that hard. Truth is, I didn't have a clue."

"Most parents probably feel that way."

How typical that everyone thinks they're the exception to the rule. "I can see that with newborns crying all the time but Simon isn't a baby. I assumed so long as he was fed, clothed and watched, things would go smoothly." He lowered his head and stared at his hands. "I never considered the problems with nightmares, day care and school-ing." The words didn't come any easier, and he was glad the night covered the heat he could feel gathering in his face. "Simon draws pictures about my lousy cooking."

"It was a good picture," she said with a deadpan expression.

Ethan smiled wryly, her sense of humor teasing his own to life. He didn't remember ever smiling as much as he had since she'd arrived. "It *was* a good picture, but it proved how Simon and I aren't connecting. You're the only person Simon's shown any interest in since he's been here, Megan. He talks to you when I can't get two words out of him. I know what Jenn said about you, but I also know everyone makes mistakes, and that kids are great judges of character, especially kids who have been through what Simon has."

A flicker of regret crossed her face, quickly followed by another weak smile of thanks. "The stuffed animal wasn't a big deal. I had one when I was his age, and Simon looked so little in that bed."

Surely Megan wouldn't turn the job offer down? She couldn't, not when Simon responded to her, smiled more. Jenn would be upset with him. Hell, she'd be furious, but wasn't Simon's health more important than hurt feelings over a boyfriend stolen years ago? Family was family. "Then let me put it this way. I've called every reputable day care in the area and toured some of the not so great ones. They're all full."

"Ah, so this isn't about helping me and Jenn but the fact that you're still desperate for child care?"

"It's both. The situation would be to both our advan-tages. You'd have a job, a home and be in close proximity to the sister you say you want to get to know again." Okay, so that was low, but some carrots had to be dangled.

Still, Megan was quiet so long he wondered if she was going to turn him down.

"How do I know you're not going to come knocking on my door in the middle of the night for extra benefits to go with the babysitting?" she finally asked with a defiant lift of her chin.

He thought that over a moment, trying to find it in him to assure her that wasn't even a thought but unable to do so. "How do I know you won't be knocking on mine?" he asked instead, giving her a slow smile. "It's been known to happen."

Humor lit her eyes at his teasing, and he saw another glimpse of the spunky, flirtatious girl she'd probably been as a teen. He stared, fascinated, much more than was wise under the circumstances. She was such a combination of vulnerability and fire. And truth be told, he wouldn't mind if she came knocking.

"Jenn will throw a fit. She won't like it."

"Nick can handle Jenn. My concern is Simon." *And you.* He didn't want her taking off when he knew she had nowhere to go. People disappeared that way, women especially. And if her sticking around meant keeping his hands off her, he'd resign himself to long, cold showers. It didn't appeal, but that was a problem he could work out later. "Do you accept?"

"Yeah. Yeah, I'll do it."

He held out his hand and waited until Megan placed her palm in his. Small, soft, the strength of her grip was surprising, but it comforted him and erased his doubts. This was the right decision, the right nanny for Simon.

The right woman for him?

Chapter 12

MEGAN NEGLECTED to cover her mouth when she yawned and stared down at the *book* in front of her. Ethan was the ultimate in sexy doctor and a seemingly nice guy but was this anal, or what?

After agreeing to take the job, Megan had come inside to watch television and distance herself from tall, dark and sexy, while Ethan had spent the evening on the computer pecking away like a two-fingered geek. She'd thought he was working on all the paperwork he'd brought home, but no. No, Ethan had been putting together a schedule for Simon.

And you. You'd certainly never keep it straight otherwise.

The list of classes and instructions was long and tedious. Most were hogwash.

Simon was to be up, fed and dressed by seven-thirty. The morning was to be spent going over flash—*can-we-say-boring?*—cards, to teach Simon basic words. Next came scheduled playtime with an emphasis on learning—it was underlined *and* highlighted. Simon was to pick up all the toys and items used and place them in the organizational bins when they were done—morning snack time, more schooling, lunch, half an hour of educational television such as PBS, Nick Jr. or NOGGIN. Then she was to take Simon to story hour at the library, bring him back home for chores and dinner, then it was on to soccer practice or one of the other sports activities Ethan had enrolled the kid in.

"Are you kidding me?" Megan stared down at the pages in her hand, one for every day this month, filled from top to bottom, beginning at eight and ending at eight when Simon went to bed.

She flipped the page, discovering a sticky note was stuck to the bottom of the food plan. A *food* plan?

Just do what you can until you're feeling better. As you can see, most of the classes start in a couple days. ET

Yeah, well, E.T. phone home and get a clue.

Simon was booked heavier than a politician the month before election. Was Ethan serious?

Soccer, swimming, story hour three times a week at the library, two group playdates with a group called Single Siblings that were held at the Y and a karate class, all there in full-color-coded detail. "Un-freaking-believable." When did the kid get a chance to breathe?

Megan glared at the pages, reminded of the schedule she'd had growing up and growing angrier with every passing second. Poor Simon!

She glanced at Simon and noticed the child had finished his toast and juice and was now eating the grapes Ethan had left.

Yup, there they were. Grapes. Right on schedule. Did Ethan expect Simon to poop on schedule, too? Was that allowed if it wasn't on the page?

She snorted. Sexy or not, had the man ever heard of spontaneity?

She couldn't blame Ethan entirely, though, if the computer signature at the bottom of the menu was any indication. The list had been put together by a dietician at the hospital where Ethan worked—*obviously another anal-retentive person*—named Candi.

Megan muttered under her breath. Really, were all those smiley faces necessary? Like that made *prunes* for breakfast any easier to stomach? Simon was five, not eighty-five.

Simon hadn't liked the half bagel or the cream cheese listed as this morning's breakfast requirement, but thankfully Ethan had left for work before he'd figured that out. So, she'd fixed the old tried-and-true along with a bowl of Cheerios with a big spoonful of sugar. Hey, at least the kid was eating. Ethan didn't have to know, right?

She tossed the pages loaded into a three-ring binder —*really, there was such a thing as being too organized*—aside and rolled her eyes.

"Qu'est-ce qu'il y a?"

"Nothing. Nothing's wrong." *Your father just has issues.* "Dr. Ethan says we have to get serious. You went to school in Niger?"

A small nod was her answer. Okay, so maybe if Simon was used to school this wouldn't be so bad? "According to this, you have flash cards Dr. Ethan bought for you? Paper with letters and pictures on them?"

Lowering his head, Simon nodded again.

Oh, yeah. There was a kid excited about the day.

Megan shook her head, wondering if Ethan would be testing Simon at the end of the week to see if she'd done any of the stuff on the schedule.

Sighing, she shoved herself away from the table. "It's too pretty outside to be stuck in here. How about we take your flash cards out and see if we can find some of the things on them?"

Simon lifted his head, his eyes sparkling with anticipation, a little grin hovering over his mouth. He liked being outside, the smile proved it. Unbidden, she laughed. He was just too cute. And easy to please. "Come on, sugar. Are you finished with your breakfast? Let's put these away and find those cards."

Simon got up, took his plate and little cup to the sink then walked to a corner of the kitchen. He opened up the pantry doors and inside Megan saw a series of storage containers stacked three high and three across in perfect rows. She stilled at the sight. Those weren't there two nights ago when she'd gone searching for a snack. When had Ethan done that?

It's a quirk. Everybody has quirks. He's not Sean.

So why did this feel so strange?

Because you're not a neat-freak. This is normal for him.

Maybe. But Ethan…Was Ethan that way, too? Sean could put on a good show whenever he wanted to. He could be charming and sweet and was the husband to have according to their friends. How much did she really know about Ethan?

Stop it. That car driving by earlier was nothing. Some guy too egotistical to ask for directions, a real estate agent taking pictures of houses, somebody's long-lost brother. It was a coincidence, nothing more. Stop making up trouble when there isn't any.

The sharp chime of the doorbell sounded, startling her so badly that she gasped, her hand flying to her chest as though it could slow the rapid pace of her heart. "It's a doorbell, Megs. Sheesh. Get a grip already."

The man driving by?

The chime rang through the house again.

Megan took a step but hesitated, dread uncoiling in her

stomach. Uneasy, Megan indicated silence to Simon by placing a finger to her lips. "Stay here."

Simon's forehead wrinkled in concern, but he nodded his understanding. Megan could tell that her indication to hush had made him worry and she felt bad for that. "It's okay, sugar. Just stay in the kitchen. I'll be right back."

Megan made her way into the living room and peeked out the window, blinking at the sight of her Buick parked in the drive. Nick's muscular form took up most of the porch. And low and behold, he was alone.

Oh, Jenn's not going to like this.

Quite frankly she didn't like it, either. Why was Nick here? Megan unlocked and opened the door but didn't invite Nick in for propriety's sake—if only Jenn was here to see *that*.

Nick's eyes were shaded by dark sunglasses but he lifted his chin in greeting. "Feeling better?"

"Yes."

"Good." He held up her key ring. "You left the keys in it."

"Thank you. That was nice of you."

"The tank is full, and I replaced the window, a few belts and added oil. You're good to go."

In other words, hit the road. "That was nice of you. I'll, um, pay you back when I can."

"No need."

"And why is that?"

"Jenn is upset about you being here. I don't like it."

Oh, he didn't like it? Poor thing! Megan opened her mouth to respond when she heard a noise behind her and saw Simon sneaking out of the kitchen. The boy ran to the recliner and hid, peeking out from behind the leather back like a miniature Rambo. Her heart stuttered in her chest.

"Simon, it's okay. Come here, sugar. It's your uncle

Nick." She waved the reluctant little boy over to her side. "Can you say hello?"

Nick squatted down and held up his hand for Simon to give him a high five. "How you doing, kiddo? Come on, now, don't leave me hanging."

Catching Nick's teasing tone and her nod that all was okay even if it wasn't, Simon gave Jenn's husband a shy smile and slapped his small hand into Nick's much larger one.

"There you go." Nick rubbed his hand over Simon's head playfully as he straightened.

"Um…yeah, so thanks again. I won't keep you."

Nick smirked, still not removing those darn sunglasses so she could see his eyes.

"You sleepin' with Ethan?"

Her mouth dropped open. "*No*. But even if I was, that's none of your business—or Jenn's." Megan braced her left shoulder and leg behind the edge of the door, although why she bothered she wasn't sure. Nick was big, imposing and downright frightening when he scowled the way that he was. If he wanted in the house, there was little she could do to stop him.

Nick's frown deepened, but he acknowledged her words with a slight nod of his head. "Fine, but I'm telling you now that you'd better not hurt them." He tilted his head toward Simon. "You're well enough to leave, even if it's just to drive to the next town. I'll give you enough money for food and a hotel for a month. Maybe a little longer if you don't blow it."

The air left her lungs in a rush. She resented Nick's presence and his opinion of her, not to mention his totally trying to manipulate the situation. "I'm not here to hurt Jenn or anyone else."

"You can't blame us for questioning your motives."

Us? Oh, yeah, that family thing. Man, what would it be like to belong to a family like that? Protective, loyal? A bittersweet longing unfurled in her chest, sharp and painful. "No, I suppose I can't. Still, that's funny because Jenn's always said she's forgiven me but it sure doesn't seem like it."

"You're smart enough to know forgiveness and trust are two different things."

"So that's why you've come to warn me away?"

"Only if you're here to hurt her."

"Look, I'll tell you what I told her, okay? What I want is a new start with my sister. I'd like to put the past behind us and move on, but how can we do that when she won't talk to me? You're here huffing and puffing in her defense, but where is she?"

His mouth tightened, and for a moment Megan wondered if she'd hit a sore spot with him. Had he been trying to get Jenn to talk to her? Megan straightened. Could it be true?

She could feel Nick's gaze dissecting her from behind his darkly tinted sunglasses, knew he watched to see if she was pulling a fast one. Her heart thudded hard in her chest but she didn't back down, didn't blink.

After a long, tense minute passed, the smallest, slightest of smiles tugged at Nick's hard-looking mouth. "You're more alike than either of you realize, aren't you?"

"Better not let her hear you say that."

His smile grew even more and for a second she could see what Jenn liked in Nick, mostly because the grin softened his features and made him look more like the ever doable Ethan.

Oh, you did not just think that.

But it was true. Ethan was much nicer looking with his dark hair and gorgeous eyes. She imagined he gave the nurses a thrill just by walking by. And now that she was feeling better, she'd admit to a thrill or two, too.

Even though it would be a huge mistake to do your boss? Weren't you the one telling Ethan the ground rules?

"So you're prepared to stick it out?"

Nick's challenge drew her out of her daze. That's it? He was going to give her a chance? "I agreed to a job here, didn't I?"

Seconds ticked by. "Want some advice?"

"Do I have a choice?"

"Not much. Jenn needs time to see this side of you. You hurt her in a bad way and now you have to prove you won't do it again."

"That's hardly a news report. How do I do that when she won't talk to me?"

He nodded toward Simon. "Don't screw up this job. Prove you're responsible. Keep calling her. If you stick it out, Jenn will come around."

"But?" She knew there had to be one.

He finally took off his glasses, his silver-blue eyes intense and direct. "But you have to be here when she's ready to talk. Screw up, and you prove your sister was right about you all along."

Chapter 13

ETHAN BROKE the speed limits as he drove out to the ball fields a week later, cursing when he met several cars he recognized. He couldn't have missed it. Simon's first soccer game?

Other members of his family were supposed to have turned out for tonight's match. How would it look that he'd missed it? Simon's age group was the first in the lineup then his nephew Matt's game was scheduled to take place after that.

Ethan spotted a familiar vehicle heading toward him and recognized his father behind the wheel. Aw, hell. His mom and dad were on their way home, meaning *both* games were over. And his excuse?

Paperwork. What kind of lousy excuse is that?

It would have been different if he'd been in surgery, but pushing a pencil and playing referee between the nursing staff and surgeons wasn't why he'd gone to medical school.

It's not all administrative. You're in charge. You own the surgery unit.

But he'd missed Simon's game. His first game.

Ethan turned around and headed home, guilt riding him hard. He pulled into the driveway, noting Megan had already pulled the blinds so he couldn't see in the windows. What was it with her and windows, anyway? She had a habit of gazing out from behind the blinds, just…looking. A habit born of her marriage?

Worry about Simon, not Megan's habits. He frowned at the clock on his dash. Was Simon still awake? It was past his bedtime, so probably not.

Ethan let himself into the house. Two steps down the hallway from the garage, he frowned. Simon's shoes weren't in the closet. He picked them up and put them away. Then he saw the socks. One here, one there, the bottom stained with grass and mud.

He grabbed those up and carried them to the utility/laundry room, placing them in a plastic container and spraying them with stain remover, all the while reminding himself that Megan was still recovering her strength and she had to be exhausted after such a long day. She'd get the hang of things soon.

Ethan started down the hall again only to stop and swear at the condition of the bathroom. Towels hung over the shower rod, bath toys littered the floor and there were two puddles by the tub. But what caught his attention was the sight of Simon's shorts—with a big wet stain on the front. "Dammit."

"You're home."

Ethan swung around and saw Megan standing just beyond Simon's bedroom door, looking thoroughly pissed yet wary.

"How did he do?"

"He wouldn't leave my side and he spent the entire game looking for you."

Ethan closed his eyes and ran a hand over his head,

squeezing the tight muscles at his neck. He wanted Simon to bond with him and the first thing he did was let Simon down. "I got behind at work and—"

"You missed his game. His *first* game."

Like he didn't know that? Hadn't he made the entire trip home swearing at himself for not being there? "I know. The time got away from me, but I'll make it up to him tomorrow." Somehow.

"Ethan, Simon doesn't even want to play but you signed him up and then you didn't show up."

"Dammit, I *know*. I'll apologize to him tomorrow."

She took a step back, looking away. In a low voice he barely heard, she said, "It would've helped if you'd called to tell him you weren't going to make it."

Ethan looked at the stain on the red shorts lying on the floor, guilt eating him alive. That's what a good parent would've done, wasn't it? Called, checked on the child. Made sure everything was under control. But he hadn't called, not once the entire day, even though he knew babysitting wasn't Megan's normal job. Megan was used to waiting tables, not handling children. What kind of parent didn't check on their kid when they knew that was the case?

One so buried in work he hadn't eaten the whole day because he couldn't afford to lose the time. "He had an accident?"

Megan rubbed her hands up and down her arms as though she was chilled. "He was so disappointed I let him stay outside and play. But when it started getting dark, I think he got scared because you still weren't home."

"There are nights I won't come home at all because I'll be on call. My schedule is unpredictable."

"Then you need to explain that to Simon. He was very upset because when you left this morning, you promised him you'd be there. Simon needs something he can depend on. Some*one* he can depend on. As his father, Ethan, you're it."

The weight on his shoulders grew heavier. Ethan took a step and mud crunched under his shoe. It was going to take him all night to clean this up. "Where did the mud come from? Simon's cleats weren't that dirty."

She pushed the hair from her face and he noted that her hand trembled.

Jenn would have been at the game tonight to watch Matt play. Had they talked? Had Jenn ignored Megan? Looking at Megan's strained features, he'd guess the latter.

Maybe this was too much, too soon. She was still recovering. As a doctor he should have been more compassionate and remembered how long it took to recover, considering how sick she'd been. He'd asked too much of her because of his desperation. Trying to see his patients, trying to take over as Chief, trying to be a parent and not doing any of it well.

"You wanted him to practice numbers today. It was in that *book* of instructions. So all day we've been counting. When we got home Simon was restless and upset, so we went outside to play and I had him count rocks and cups of dirt, and we made mud pies."

Mud pies? Unease filled him. Anger. "I spent a fortune on toys. There are blocks in the bins he could've counted."

Megan backed up a step. "We counted those earlier today. Look, you had counting all over that stupid schedule," she added defensively, "so we *counted*."

He followed her, noting that with every step he took, she backed up another. The sight of her scooting away from him so that he had to chase her down to talk frustrated the hell out of him. Where was she going? "That's fine. I don't care how he learns the things he needs to learn, but I don't want Simon playing in mud."

She crossed her arms over her front, but retreated again. "Every kid plays in mud. Are you that much of a snob? I took his shoes off."

"It's not about his shoes, Megan."

"Then what is it about? Stop taking your bad mood out on me because you're feeling guilty about tonight. Simon had fun until it started getting dark, then he got scared because you weren't home."

"Maybe that was it, or it could've been because he was worried since you hadn't set the mud to dry and the sun was going down. It takes a while for it to harden."

"Harden?" She stared at him, her face a mask of confusion. "We weren't making anything, we were just playing."

"You were playing, Simon was surviving." He lifted both hands to his head, raking his fingers through his hair, his thoughts on Simon and what she'd said. "Megan, Simon was hungry."

"What?"

Ethan released the air in his lungs in a rush, squeezing and rubbing his neck harder to ease the tension that wouldn't let up. "It's not your fault. You couldn't have known."

"Known *what?*"

"Simon probably thought you were making dinner. Dirt cookies. It's what the villagers eat when they don't have anything else. A little water, some salt and animal fat, and dirt."

She shook her head mutely, totally aghast.

"Some of the schools use it as punishment. They feed them to the kids when they've been bad. But mostly it's used by parents when they can't stand to hear their hungry children crying."

"You mean Simon thought he'd been bad and—Oh, my—*Oh*." Her hand flew to her mouth and she rushed by him, gagging.

Ethan followed her into the bathroom, getting there in time to see Megan fall to her knees and lose the contents of her stomach. Cursing himself because he knew Megan well enough to know she'd react this way, he got a cloth and wet it, pressing it to her neck with one hand while he gathered her hair with the other.

When it was over she was shaking so badly he sat with his back against the tub and settled her next to him on the cool tile floor. Surprisingly, she stayed put. "Better?"

She nodded weakly, her face pasty white. Her lashes were wet and spiky, and her mascara had smeared beneath her eyes. No woman should still look beautiful after that.

"I had n-no idea."

He forced his thoughts back to the topic at hand. "Most people don't, especially not here in the States, unless they lived through the Depression. I guess the recipe is an old one."

Megan sniffled, her fingers fussing with the edges of the cloth until she lifted her head and turned to face him. "I fed him dinner. After his bath. We'd had hot dogs at the game and I wasn't hungry so I assumed he wasn't." She closed her eyes and shook her head in obvious upset. "I made soup and grilled cheese sandwiches and he ate every bite. I should've realized then but…"

The words were defensive and full of self-loathing, and Ethan smoothed his hand over her back once more. He didn't remember the soup and sandwich combo on the schedule, much less hot dogs, but he wasn't about to argue. The food program was an attempt to get Simon's weight up to scale but so long as he was eating, one slip every now and again wouldn't hurt. "That's good."

"How can you say that? If I made Simon think he'd been bad, if that's why he had the accident—I blamed it on you getting home late and Simon getting scared, but it was because of *me*." She squeezed her eyes shut with a moan. "Oh, I can just see your brother's face when he hears about this."

"Which brother? Nick?"

She nodded, looking completely dejected as she sniffled and turned her head to hide the tears in her eyes. "He challenged me to prove to Jenn that I could do it, but this proves—"

"Nothing." He squeezed her close to his side, shifting so that he could lift her face and she had to look at him. "Megan? It proves nothing. It's okay. Yes, it is," he insisted when she tried to shake her head no. "Anyone could've made the mistake you made. I made mud pies all the time as a kid. Tonight you proved to Simon that he could play in the mud and still have food and he wasn't being punished. You fed him at the game, right? So maybe he was a little hungry but he wasn't starving. He's safe and sound now, right?"

She nodded, quiet, still trembling and completely horrified by what she'd done, however unintentionally.

They sat that way for a while, side by side on the uncomfortable floor, Megan's head on his shoulder. He massaged her arm, her shoulder, not stopping until the light, easy strokes eased the tension from her body and began to create another one altogether in his.

He stared at the wall across from them. Tonight was a mistake, one any babysitter could have made. He couldn't blame Megan for not understanding the extreme poverty in Niger since he hadn't understood it until going there himself. It upset him to think Simon might have thought he was being punished, but sitting there with Megan resting against him, he knew the boy would be fine.

Megan's reaction to her blunder ended any residual doubts he might have had about her care of Simon, her personality and her heart. Megan wasn't an expert with kids and neither was he. They'd muddle their way through this together and pray Simon would forgive them the mistakes they made along the way.

"Dirt cookies?"

He pressed a kiss to the top of her head before he realized it was inappropriate. Just like holding her all this time was inappropriate. But she wasn't pulling away and he wasn't about to suggest it, not when he'd been interested in Megan from the moment he'd laid eyes on her in Nick's backyard. He looked down at her, realized her shirt had ridden up just a tad and he spotted the glint of her belly piercing.

"It's, um, *ahem*, all in the ratio. They don't taste too horrible if there's enough salt and fat in them."

Meg looked up at him. Her face expressed her heartache on Simon's behalf, on behalf of anyone hungry enough to be that desperate. He tried not to dwell on it, knowing he could only do so much. But the doctor in him raged at the injustice. Over a billion people in the world were overweight, but the exact same amount of people were starving. Amazing how some had all, some had nothing.

From the looks of things, Megan not only sympathized, she felt the same pain he did at the thought of so many children like Simon going hungry. It was another point on his list of must-haves in the women he dated—compassion.

He was pleased to note Megan had it in spades.

With the house quiet and Megan in his arms, he fought

the ever-stronger pull of attraction, something elemental and base and strong with desire. He and Megan had forged a bond tonight, one made by their feelings for the child asleep in the other room.

Don't go there. She's great with Simon. Don't screw up a good thing.

Messing around with Megan would be the ultimate in stupidity. Jenn wouldn't like it but that wasn't his problem. No, the problem was that Megan was right. Simon needed a constant in his life. And Ethan's schedule being what it was, *Megan* was the constant. She related to Simon in a way Ethan couldn't, and a physical relationship with her could potentially ruin everything. What kind of father would he be to mess up Simon's future in exchange for sex?

Simon aside, should Megan and Jenn repair their relationship, he could also find himself facing Megan periodically after their encounter ended and that would be insanely awkward.

But it would be fun.

He bit back a halfhearted groan, feeling like his old self again for the first time since leaving for Niger. Yeah, it would be fun. For as scrawny as she was, Megan defined sex—except for the part where she'd hurled.

"Come on," he said, standing to put some distance between them only to reach a hand down to help her to her feet. Her palm felt small and soft and strong, and it was all he could do not to think of her touching him in other places. "I'm hungry. Let's go replace the dinner you just lost."

Chapter 14

MEGAN HELD SIMON'S HAND as they headed toward My Kid's Closet, unable to shake the feeling that something was off. She hadn't been out of the house much since her arrival, but now that she was strolling along Main Street and her neck tingled with unease, she wished she'd stayed home.

Before leaving for work this morning, Ethan had asked how she was feeling and if she was up to doing a little shopping. Considering she loved to shop and hadn't been able to do any for a while due to her financial situation, she'd jumped at the chance to take Simon to town to purchase winter clothes. The days were starting to cool down and the weatherman had stated just this morning that it would be in the fifties one day next week.

Her neck prickled again, and Megan paused and scanned the area, not seeing anything out of the ordinary and hating the knot in her stomach that formed. *Paranoid*, her inner voice taunted in a singsong voice. *You've been on edge so long you're losing it. This is your one safe place, remember?*

She led Simon to the corner and waited for the cross-

IVY JAMES

signal, the tingling sensation spreading down her spine and the knot growing larger like a balloon about to burst. Was she being watched?

You're a new face in a small town. Of course you're being watched. Every gossip on the street is probably on their phone right now, trying to figure out who you are and why you're with Ethan Tulane's son. Get used to it.

It hadn't taken long to figure out the Tulane name carried a lot of weight. Sitting on the sidelines of the soccer game she'd had several people come introduce themselves to her just because she'd had Simon in tow and they'd heard of his adoption.

The light changed and she tugged Simon across to the other side, the breeze carrying a bit of coolness with it. Did Simon have a winter coat? He'd need one soon. Maybe a snowsuit, too, since Ethan said every now and again they got snow in the mountains. She'd have to ask Ethan, or else just add it to the bill today and return it if her employer protested the expense.

You weren't thinking of him as an employer last night.

Heat surged up her neck and into her face at the memory of Ethan holding her. It had felt so good to be comforted after that horrible mistake. Ethan had had every right to be furious with her, reason enough to fire her. Instead of yelling at her and kicking her out the door, he'd held her. Yet another way Ethan proved he wasn't like Sean.

Simon walked beside her, wide-eyed as he took in the buildings, the flags flapping in the breeze and the mix of leftover Halloween decorations competing with Christmas sale signs. Given Simon's shyness, Ethan had skipped the Halloween trick-or-treat ritual last weekend and opted to spend a quiet night at home.

A bell jingled as they stepped over the threshold of the

134

shop. A gigantic stuffed giraffe towered over them, colorful clothes filled the space and a whole display of stuffed animals lined half of one wall, but the sight of the older woman wearing a name tag heading their way was enough to make Megan clutch Simon's hand a wee bit tighter.

"You must be Megan Rose. I'm Mrs. Stouts. And this must be little Simon. Hello, Simon," she said, enunciating each syllable like an old record album played on slow speed.

The woman bent, placing her hands on her knees, and bobbed up and down several times. The sight made Megan wonder if the woman was about to break into a dance routine or a game of Simon Says.

"Your, um, *father*," she said, drawing out the word until it became *fah-thur*, "asked me to help you find some nice clothes." She addressed Megan next, straightening. "After all, little Simon needs to be dressed appropriately, what with Dr. Tulane being who he is."

Who he is? If she'd learned anything about Ethan since staying with him, it was that he didn't care what he wore so long as it was clean and comfortable. Ethan was the last one to throw around the fact he sliced people open on a regular basis.

The conversation they'd had when she'd first arrived came back to her, the one about how Ethan just wanted to do his job, be who he was, and not have the hassle of living up to some kind of expectation. So because Ethan was a doctor, he was expected to dress Simon a certain way, was that it?

Get off your high horse. You know what she means.

That she did. When she'd done the pageant circuit, it was expected that the participants have certain brands of clothing, a certain style. This was no different. "We, um, don't have a lot of time. Just point me in the right direction and I'll find what we need."

"Oh, nonsense, dear. I'll be with you every step of the way. I've taken the liberty of gathering some things together for Simon already. Just follow me."

I can't wait. Megan's eye twitched when she spotted a glittery sea of pageant gowns, prom gowns and winter dance numbers up ahead. Those were followed by leotards, dance, tap and ballet shoes.

The portion of stock dedicated to boys was in the back of the store and after meandering around the racks rather than taking the direct path, they finally made it.

"Here we are. We have just the things for you, little man."

The curtained dressing room was spacious, with three mirrors and a bench. Already hanging on hooks were half a dozen jeans and shirts, flannel pajamas, two black suits, a tuxedo, a brown suit and at least six dress shirts. Surely Mrs. Stouts didn't expect Simon to try on all of that?

Simon stared up at Megan, his expression pleading for them to turn and bolt. *So with ya, kid.*

Megan let go of his hand and knelt down beside him, her voice low as she told him in French, "The sooner we do this, the sooner we leave. Once we're finished we'll go home and do something *very* special, okay?"

"Oh! You speak *French!* Oh, my word, what a find Dr. Tulane has in you! Why, wait until I tell my friend Doris. She's been looking for someone to tutor her daughter in French. There's this song she wants to sing in Beauty's Winterfest pageant and—"

"I'm not a tutor." She gave Simon a reassuring wink and straightened. "I'm just visiting my family and helping out with Simon."

"Oh, but—Rose," the woman said abruptly, her gaze

narrowing like a bargain shopper in sight of sales. "Wasn't that the name of the woman Dr. Tulane's brother married? Nick? He dated my daughter a time or two. She was runner-up in the Miss Tennessee Pageant."

"How nice." They were never going to get out of here at this rate.

"Yes, it was. There's her picture, there on the wall." She pointed to a framed photo of a woman with big hair and enough eye makeup to make a clown jealous. Megan so didn't miss those days.

"Oh, now who was that girl he married? Julie or Jenna —*Jennifer!* That's it, Jennifer Rose, the teacher. I remember seeing it in the paper." The woman sniffed. "She bought her gown in Nashville. My Amanda was working in the shop with me then. Mandy's so pretty, I think she intimidates the customers."

Just pick something. Simon can try it on later. "What's your return policy?"

"Probably intimidated that girl he married, too, not that I could blame her. My Mandy would be a hard act to follow." The woman looked her up and down. "You're related? Cousins, perhaps?"

"Jenn's my little sister."

"Your sister? Really? And younger, too," she murmured with a frown. "Imagine that. Oh, honey, don't get me wrong, but I remember your sister before she lost weight. Not to be mean, but—well, everyone wondered *why* Nick chose her."

Megan realized this was one of those times when somebody was watching. God, *Candid Camera*, Grandma Lucy, who'd *always* told her and Jenn to not say anything at all if they couldn't say something nice. That feeling of being watched earlier? This was why. Somebody somewhere was waiting to see if Megan ripped Mrs. Stouts a new one. "Maybe Nick chose her because Jenn is a kind, generous and loving person, and he's in love with her."

Megan was about to give herself a pat on the back for making Grandma Lucy smile down on her from Heaven when Mrs. Stouts made a face. One of those pretend-to-be-nice-but-really-a-shark faces women like her so often wore.

"All I'm saying is that there is quite a difference. I mean, look at you. You're beautiful."

Meaning Jenn wasn't? That stinking knot in her stomach burned. At this rate she'd have an ulcer. Was this what Jenn had dealt with growing up? Their father had always made comments to them about each other, played them off one another to divert attention from himself and his exploits with his flavor of the moment, but she'd never given much thought to whether or not outsiders compared them. "I think Jenn is beautiful. She has the most fabulous hourglass figure and perfect skin."

Mrs. Stouts finally seemed to wise up to the fact that Megan wasn't going to tear Jenn down or talk about her behind her back. *Another star in your crown, Megs.*

"Oh, pay me no mind. It's just that you're so thin and, well, I've heard Nick keeps Jennifer on a strict diet. I feel sorry for the poor girl."

What? Megan was about to grab Simon's hand and head for the door out of sheer frustration, knowing full well Ethan wouldn't mind her not buying clothes for Simon here because of the gossip's focus being on a member of his family, but instead she lifted a hand and indicated the curtain. "Could we have some privacy, please?"

"Of course."

She pulled the material into place and took a deep

breath, knowing the woman hadn't budged an inch. "A diet, you say?"

"Oh, yes. How do you think she's lost all that weight?"

All that weight? Megan froze in the act of settling Simon on the bench in preparation for unlacing his shoes.

"Everyone's seen how he has her doing that power walking and working out in the gym. I heard she even fainted once because he was pushing her so hard on an exercise bike. Mandy said he was like that when they dated. She wanted him to do some things with his family, but instead he'd go work out like something possessed."

Kind of like Ethan's cleaning? She'd honestly thought Ethan employed a housekeeper the first week she was there, but now she knew he didn't. He was the one scrubbing away at all hours of the night. How many times had she gone to bed thinking she'd straighten up in the morning only to find it done—regardless of what time Ethan had gotten home? The dirt tracked in from making mud pies, the towels and toys.

Megan gripped Simon's ankle so tight, the boy squirmed and pulled away from her. "Sorry, sugar." She rubbed his ankle to soothe it then set to work on the other shoe.

Cleaning was one thing, but Nick had another think coming if he thought he'd get away with treating Jenn like his personal diet pet. "She actually passed out?"

"*Yes.* Right there in the middle of the gym. Folks said he had his head down and was nose to nose with her, saying awful things and glaring at her. But, now, I'm not a gossip."

"Of course not," Megan said softly, playing along because she had to know what was going on but glad she was behind the curtain and Mrs. Stouts couldn't see her face. "I'm her sister. I need to know these things and I appreciate your confiding in me."

Was Jenn in trouble? Did Nick have control issues like Sean? What kind of family had her baby sister married into? *Oh, Jenn. What did Dad do to us?*

"That's true. Family is family. Don't say I told you this but I heard…"

ETHAN HURRIED DOWN the hospital hallway, his thoughts on Megan. What were she and Simon doing now? Had they gone shopping? Was Megan having fun picking things out for Simon? He should have told her to get a sweater or something for herself, even though she probably would have bristled like a porcupine. He'd never known a woman to be so hard to read. Sometimes she was flirtatious, sometimes leery, sometimes happy then wary.

He knew it had to do with her past but it made her moods hard to decipher, much less follow. He'd never lived with a woman, never wanted to, but he was more than a little fascinated by everything Megan did.

Ethan glanced at his watch and swore. Late for yet another meeting. When had life become all about paperwork and meetings? Turning a corner, he ran smack into his brother Garret. "Sorry."

"Where's the fire?"

Ethan glanced around and lowered his voice. "Apparently up the new administrative chief of staff's ass. I was headed to surgery and had to find someone to cover for me because Gibson has decided we need to meet to discuss some new policy. You know, ever since you left, that joker has been pulling power trips."

"And now as interim chief, you get to deal with them."

Garret smirked. "When Harry was the hospital's president he pulled his power trips on me, but I was nice enough not to pass them on."

"Yeah, yeah, rub it in. How lucky I'm the one with two new guys who like to spread the wealth. You know, you could come back and settle things down. You'd be welcomed with open arms." Ethan continued walking down the corridor and Garret fell into step beside him.

"Not a chance. I'm happy sharing office space with Tobe," Garret said, referring to his law practice with his friend Tobias Richardson. "How's Simon?"

Ethan checked the time and frowned. Late was late. "I don't know how you do this parent thing. I can't imagine diapers and midnight feedings with a kid who can't tell you what she wants. It's bad enough with a five-year-old who refuses to tell you."

"He'll come around once he gets used to you. And you'll get used to him and be able to read his moods. But you'd better not get into the habit of missing Simon's games or else you're going to have Mom and Dad both coming down on you. You owe Nick, by the way. Anytime Dad brought up your absence, Nick changed the subject and got him going on something else."

Thank God. Now that Alan Tulane was considering retirement, he was constantly giving his children lectures on the things he'd done wrong when they were growing up. Their father was bound and determined his children wouldn't make the same mistakes he had. "What was said about Megan?"

"A lot. She sat on the sidelines instead of with us in the stands, but Jenn told Darcy you'd be lucky if you weren't robbed blind and left tied to the bed. Hate to tell you this, but Mom heard."

"Crap."

"So what's Megan's story? I've heard bits and pieces. What's your take?"

"She sincerely wants to make things up with Jenn, but Jenn doesn't trust her."

"And you do?"

He thought about that a moment then nodded firmly. "I wouldn't leave Simon with her if I didn't. Simon loves her and after everything the kid's been through he's a great judge of character."

Garret accepted that with a nod. "So, does that mean you and Megan are playing doctor?"

Ethan stopped so abruptly Garret took two more steps before he realized Ethan wasn't beside him. "She's Jenn's sister and my son's nanny."

"So? Wait a minute…. *Are* you?"

The thought alone sent his blood pressure into orbit. "Of course not. She's helping me out with Simon because I gave her a place to stay when Jenn wouldn't." But something didn't ring true about his denial and Garret picked up on it by the way he raised his eyebrow.

Ethan blamed the thongs. He'd done a load of laundry and found one of Megan's thongs left behind in the dryer. Skimpy and black; he'd had a hard time getting the image of her wearing it out of his head. And after holding her in his arms, his restraint was wearing thin.

Going home was a pleasure. The way the house smelled when he opened the door, like Megan's perfume and whatever she'd fixed for dinner. He liked how they'd put Simon to bed, and then Megan would crash on the couch and watch television while he plowed through the mountains of paperwork that never ended. It was nice. Nicer than he'd ever thought it could be, even though he went to bed and stared at the ceiling thinking of thongs and belly piercings and how good she'd taste. He'd had offers, too. Hospitals were a regular soap opera when it came to sex and hooking up, but not a single woman there appealed the way Megan did.

"So what exactly happened between her and Jenn?"

Ethan exhaled in a rush and wondered how he could explain then wanted to smack himself in the head for his lapse in thinking. If anyone would understand, it was Garret since his best friend and partner was now married to Garret's former girlfriend. Ethan gave Garret the two-second version and waited for the words to sink in.

His brother's frown deepened at the convoluted story. "What does Nick say about it?"

"Dunno. I've been so busy I haven't had a chance to talk to him again. But I think it's going to take all of us to figure out a way of getting Megan and Jenn back on good terms. It's only fair, seeing as how Jenn brought Nick back."

"Only fair, huh?" Garret clapped Ethan on the shoulder. "And if we get them on good terms, it wouldn't be such a problem having Megan around, would it?"

Garret had always had a way of reading between the lines—usually correctly, too. "Simon says he likes her. It might be nice if Megan could stick around."

Garret smirked and shoved Ethan onto the now-empty elevator. "Simon says, huh? You know, the ones in denial usually fall the hardest."

Chapter 15

"COME ON, ONE MORE CUP. Do it just like I did." Megan indicated the newly purchased bag of all-purpose flour with a wave of her hand. After clothes shopping they'd stopped by the grocery because Ethan's kitchen had contained all the necessary ingredients to make a special memory, except for one.

Ethan didn't want Simon playing in the dirt for fear of bad memories, so why not make good ones? Besides, stopping had given her a chance to buy a box of hair color. Her roots were in serious need of a touch-up.

Simon shook his head.

"Come on, why not?"

Simon stared at her with his big brown eyes, silent. Afraid?

She sighed and dipped into the bag for another scoop. "Three," she said, pointing to the flour in the mixing bowl. "Four." She poured the cup of flour on top of the rest. A batch of cookies for them—and one for Jenn? Cookies were a nice icebreaker. Maybe they'd get her in the door long enough to find out if Nick was emotionally or physically abusive. She had to know.

Mrs. Stouts had spent the entire hour standing outside the changing room. She'd filled Megan in on every snippet of gossip she'd heard regarding Jenn and Nick, including Nick's dropping out of high school. Megan never would have pictured her straight-A, gotta-graduate-at-the-top-of-my-class sister with a dropout but then, who knew what other people thought?

By the time Megan had left the shop she'd been on edge and sick to her stomach. What if Nick was abusing Jenn? Keeping her on a diet? *Making* her exercise? All those little things Sean and her father had done to keep Megan in her place came back to her. The comments, the looks. And that time when Sean—

Simon moved. She'd been standing there staring at him completely lost in a daze. Poor kid, he probably wondered why she glared at him when it was Sean she saw in her mind. Good memories. They were making good memories now.

"Okay," she said, focusing on the recipe card Jenn thought lost forever and shoving the past aside. "Now all we need is the baking powder and—"

She knocked over the mixing bowl.

Megan watched as the metal bowl fell to the floor in slow motion. Her hands flew to her mouth, but she couldn't stifle the horrified cry that escaped when the bowl landed with a clatter and a mushroom cloud of white exploded into the air. "No! Oh, no, oh *no.*"

She dropped to her knees, grabbed the spinning bowl and stilled it, scooping the flour into the bowl with her hands. Her hair kept getting in her face and she shoved it back, scraping, clawing, frantic.

"I didn't mean to break it. I'll clean up the mess, I'll clean it up!"

"Yeah, well what about the rest of the house?"

"It's clean!"

"Clean?" Sean snarled at her, his breath foul from too much alcohol and cheap appetizers from his favorite bar. His hand tangled in her hair, stopped her midstep, and when he yanked her back against his chest, his other hand found her throat and squeezed. "You're pathetic. I expect a clean house. Is that too much to ask after I work all day? Is it?"

"No!"

"No, it's not. When I tell you to clean the house, I expect to see you on your knees." A salacious grin formed on his too-full lips. "So let's see you, Meggie. On your knees!"

Megan flinched with the memory of what came next, a sob in her throat as she kept scooping, crawling on her hands and knees, faster, desperate, scrambling. Please, please, please. She had to get it cleaned up. Had to—

She bumped into Simon. Megan nearly toppled over the child where he knelt beside her trying just as hard to scoop up the mess, tears streaming down his face. He'd caught on to her terrified panic, repeating something in his little boy voice.

"I help. I help, Miss Megan. It okay. I help."

Megan stilled at the sight, the awful, fear-shrill sound. And the way Simon looked at her? Oh, Lord, what had she done?

She couldn't breathe, couldn't see for the tears stinging her eyes and the flour dust in the air, couldn't stop shaking. "Simon? Simon, come here. No, baby, come here." She reached for him, her hands leaving white imprints of flour on his skin. Megan pulled his sturdy boy body into her arms and held him close, burying her nose in his neck and biting her lip until it bled to keep the memories inside her, locked in a place where Simon wouldn't see. She rocked him back and forth. Rock, hug, sniffle. Rock, hug, kiss. She'd make it okay. She had to. "I'm sorry, sugar. Oh, Simon, I'm so sorry. I didn't mean to scare you. It's okay."

Megan sat on the floor for a long time, Simon on her lap with his arms wrapped tight around her neck, each of them holding on to the other while she crooned the words to him, to herself, petted and rocked and tried to make it better. Tried to make the past disappear for them both.

Simon raised his head, his mocha eyes seeing all the way to her soul.

"Miss Megan *éffrayée?*"

She sniffled and tried to brave a smile. "Miss Megan *was* afraid," she said thickly. "A long time ago I knew a mean man," she whispered in French. "He made me afraid and I—I remembered. Just for a moment. But that was a long time ago and I'm not afraid anymore. I'm sorry for frightening you."

"Je déteste les hommes méchants! Ils ont tué mon oncle."

Mean men…they killed my uncle. The whispered admission broke Megan's heart. There was such desolation in Simon's eyes, an untold horror of all he'd seen. "Oh, Simon. I know they did. I'm so sorry, sugar."

Simon reached out and grabbed the end of her hair in his fist. *"Mademoiselle Megan a l'air d'un nuage."*

"A cloud, huh?" His tears had dried in streaks on his face, but his eyes now sparkled with a hint of a smile. Thank God for short attention spans. Maybe in time Simon's memories of that horrible day would fade. She smiled back, hugged him again and kissed his flour-coated cheek. "Clouds are pretty."

Simon looked down, then reached out a finger and poked it into a hill of flour by their legs. *"Doux."*

"It is soft." And probably a lot different than what he

was used to. "It's also good to eat once it's cooked." She looked up at the clock on the stove. Plenty of time to clean up. Plenty of time to make a new batch of cookies.

Megan leaned back against the cabinets, a smile forming on her lips as she watched the solemn little boy play in the flour, fascinated by the texture and color.

Catching a glimpse of herself in the stainless-steel stove, a laugh erupted from her chest. Her hair was coated in white, her face and clothes, too. Too bad they'd missed Halloween, because they could've both gone as ghosts. "I do look like a cloud," she said, pointing at their reflection. "But you know what?"

She dropped her hand to her side and her fingers curled around a handful of flour. "So. Do. *You!*" she cried, tickling his neck and covering his cheeks and head with flour and kisses.

ETHAN SIGHED as he wiped down the wood cabinet. He'd always heard the expression about being too tired to sleep, but since his return from Niger, he lived it.

He paused in his cleaning when he heard the kitchen's swing door open behind him with a *swish* of air. Without thought he straightened from the floor near the refrigerator, and Megan shrieked, backing up so fast she hit the countertop with a bang. She winced from the impact.

"Are you okay?" He held up his hands, still holding the rag he used. "I didn't mean to scare you."

And he had. Her pulse thrummed in her throat and her chest rose and fell with her rapid breaths. She hugged her arms around her ribs and leaned heavily against the counter, one foot tucked under the other while she glared at him.

"Don't *do* that. Don't ever do that."

He frowned at the panic in her tone, the fear-glazed look in her eyes. She'd avoided him all evening, gone to bed early. Had something happened? "I'm sorry."

She lifted a hand to her face and shoved her hair out of the way. "No, it's—it's okay. I'm jumpy tonight."

"Why? Did you have another bad dream?"

Her gaze flicked to his in wary surprise. That changed to suspicion when her attention shifted to his hand.

"What are you doing?"

Her gaze focused on the rag and beneath the soft glow of the light over the sink, he saw her pale.

"I—I'm sorry. I thought I got it all."

"Does this have anything to do with that mountain of cookies over there?"

Emotions danced over her face, sadness, determination, bittersweet joy. "I felt so bad after the dirt cookie incident that I wanted to make a new memory for Simon." A small, sad smile pulled at her lips. "Our first attempt didn't go so well because I, um, accidentally dropped the bowl. Nothing broke," she rushed to reassure him, "but it made an awful mess." She reached for the rag. "Here, let me have that. I'll clean it again."

He held his hand up so that she couldn't get it. "It's fine. I'm almost done." He couldn't keep from chuckling. "I would've loved to have seen your face. I'll bet you —What?"

Megan blinked and tilted her head to one side, her face a mass of confusion, disbelief and something close to…pleasure?

"You're not mad."

She said it with absolute and total amazement. "Because you had an accident? No, sweetheart. Why would I be?"

Megan closed the distance between them in a scant second, plastered herself to his front and kissed him. Ethan told himself to keep it light, a kiss of…thanks or friendship or whatever Megan meant the gesture to be. But he was also a guy with a beautiful woman in his arms, a woman he'd wanted to taste for too damn long, and no way was he going to let the opportunity pass.

Pressing Megan closer, he returned the kiss with all the desire and curiosity inside him, plundering her mouth when she parted her lips and let him inside. This wasn't a tender, get-to-know-you peck but a raw, full-blown kiss. As a first it blew his mind, because she tasted like spearmint and rich wine and sex in a darkened kitchen.

His body went up in flames as all the blood drained from his brain to regions that hadn't seen any action in months, and he kept on kissing her, nudging her backward until her waist hit the counter and he cupped her behind, lifting, setting her on the edge with him wedged firmly between her thighs.

Ethan broke the continuous stream of kisses and trailed his lips along her jaw, lower. He nibbled and kissed the tender crook of her neck, smiling at her muffled gasp, the goose bumps that rose on her skin. Her hands gripped his shoulders, fingers digging into his T-shirt to hold him close and he continued his exploration, ignoring the voice in his head to end things now before he did something to scare her or, worse yet, ruined a phenomenal working relationship.

His hands drifted from her waist, up her sides beneath her robe but over her pajama top, thumbs brushing the outsides of her small breasts. She wore nothing underneath. Megan caught her breath and held it as he hesitated, drawing the moment out and savoring the excitement of touching her for the first time. Faces close, noses brushing, he watched Megan's lashes flutter open when he covered her breasts with his palms and gently squeezed, learning the shape, tracing the delicate tips with his thumbs. Her thighs tightened at his waist, nudging the length of him standing at full attention against the cotton-covered place he most wanted to be.

But there was something wrong. These past weeks of living together had given him more insight into her moods and this one made him leery. She seemed desperate, hurting. Trying to run away from whatever it was in her head, whatever had made her jumpy. And while he'd like nothing more than to let her use his body at will, he also knew she'd regret it come morning.

"Sweetheart, we have to stop." He breathed the words against her mouth, kissed her gently to soften the refusal and somehow made himself smooth his hands back down to her sides. He snuggled her close, pulling her into his arms and rubbing her back until the feverish need to go further burned a little less hot. "I think it's clear I want you. We'd be fantastic together," he added, not bothering to disguise the need in his husky voice.

"But Jenn's warned you to run the other way."

He nudged her chin up with a finger, pulling back to see her face. "This has nothing to do with Jenn." He dropped another kiss on her lips. "And everything to do with what's best for Simon…and you. We do this," he said, leaning into the vee of her hips and letting her feel how hard he was as a result of their play, "and there's no going back. Plus—" he smoothed his thumb over her soft lower lip "—being in Niger has changed my perspective on casual sex. HIV has a way of doing that."

"I'm safe. I was tested after…I've been tested."

He wanted to ask what she was about to say, but didn't.

"So have I. But if we do this, we don't have to be in a hurry, do we?"

He wasn't sure which of them was more surprised by his question. To suggest they could do this again later after what he'd just said meant…what? Something more serious?

"Most guys wouldn't have stopped."

"I don't want to. I want you stripped and naked," he stated bluntly, his mind picturing her that way now. "But until you can sleep in my house without having nightmares, until you can kiss me because you want to and not because you're jumpy or grateful I wasn't angry over an accident, we need to get to know each other better."

She tilted her head to the side, looking soft and sad and happy all at once. He dropped another kiss to her mouth because he couldn't help himself and sighed. "Come on. Neither one of us are tired right now. Let's go grab some of those cookies. I think there's just enough ice cream left."

Chapter 16

FIVE MINUTES LATER they were curled up on the couch. The impromptu make-out session in the kitchen should have made things awkward, but all he felt was an intense need for a repeat—soon. "I, um, remember Gram doing the same thing when I was a kid," he murmured, attempting to make small talk and follow his own advice of learning more about Megan.

"Your grandmother?"

"Yeah. She and the girls—my sister, Alex, and her best friend, Shelby—were in the kitchen baking for Christmas. There wasn't a single spot that wasn't covered by cookies or dough. It looked like an assembly line. Anyway, Alex and Shelby started arguing over something, Gram got distracted and the bowl of cookie mix hit the floor. Everyone in the house came to see what the fuss was about because they started laughing so hard."

"Sounds like a lot of fun. Your family's close?"

"Yeah, very. You'll meet the rest of them soon. At Thanksgiving, if not before."

Her smile dimmed. "I doubt Jenn will want me there."

Maybe not, but as Simon's nanny, Megan had to set aside her need for Jenn's approval and accept the fact that sometimes two people just had to agree to disagree. "I wouldn't be allowed in the door if I didn't bring you. And I want you to go." He wanted to see for himself what his family thought of Megan, if they'd accept her based on their impressions rather than Jenn's. "Don't worry about Jenn. My family takes their hosting duties very seriously," he told her with a smile, "and you'll be welcome, fed and fussed over until you can't wait to get out the door."

Megan rubbed her hands up and down her arms as though chilled, an unreadable expression on her face. "That sounds nice."

Her look of longing gave him pause. That and her envy of how close his family was in comparison to hers gave him more insight into her sincerity. "What's wrong, sweetheart?"

Her head dipped and he saw her wriggle her toes where her feet were propped on the coffee table. A flush surged into Megan's cheeks, and Ethan couldn't help but think if she was experienced at stealing boyfriends and marrying them, she should've lost the ability to blush a while ago.

"Jenn will probably accuse me of sleeping with you, especially after that crack I made about taking advantage of you. Think she'll be able to tell we…"

"Made out like teenagers?" He set his bowl of ice cream aside and put his arm around Megan's shoulders. "I don't care if she can tell. Don't let her be too hard on you. It's none of her business what we do or don't do."

"That's what I told Nick." She released the lip she worried between her teeth and smiled at him, leaning her head on his shoulder briefly before raising it again with a tentative look of trust mixed with unease. "Ethan…can I ask you something?"

With one look at her face, Ethan could tell how much impact Megan was placing on his response. "You can ask me anything, say anything and never fear the repercussions, Megan."

Ethan's heart stuttered to a halt when Megan gifted him with a beautiful smile. Her smiles had become more frequent lately, but none of them looked like the one she gave him now.

"Thanks. That means a lot."

"You're welcome. Now ask."

Whatever it was took more preparation because she inhaled deeply before saying, "I, um, took Simon to pick out some clothes like you asked. I put everything away and left the tags on, so if there's anything you don't like or think is too much, they can go back."

"I'm sure they're fine. Was there a problem at the store?"

"No." She played with the ice cream in her bowl, digging her spoon into the mix and making it into a chunky milk shake. "But someone said—that is, I heard… Is Nick abusive?"

"What?" Ethan turned to stare at her, unable to mask his surprise. "Is someone saying that? Who?"

"It doesn't matter who, what matters is if it's true."

"It's not."

"Are you sure? Do you know if Nick made Jenn work out so hard that she passed out?"

Damn. He'd suspected Megan had been ill-treated but this—He didn't like the thoughts in his head, the confirmation he saw in her eyes with her worry for Jenn. Even now Megan had a hard time looking directly at him, despite having accused his brother of hurting his wife. "Like me," he stated firmly, "Nick wouldn't hurt anyone. Sweetheart, the only way any member of my family would hurt someone is if someone they cared for was being threatened. And if that was the case, we would all do whatever was necessary to protect our own. As to what happened at the gym, I was there the day Jenn *nearly* passed out. She didn't, she just got light-headed and dizzy, but it was because she hadn't followed the diet regime and skipped breakfast."

"He has her on a regime?"

She said the words with enough disgust that Ethan's fingers tensed on her shoulder. He instantly relaxed his hand and smoothed his fingers into a massaging caress, and focused on controlling his anger reflexes until Megan knew him well enough to know she never had anything to fear from him. Still, he hated gossips and was upset by Megan's worry.

"Get the story straight," he told her, "before you jump to conclusions and judge. Small-town gossip can get ridiculously bent out of shape in no time flat. The truth is, Jenn went to Nick and asked for advice on how to lose weight. He owns the gym as well as the garage in town, and he's done a bit of personal training.

"They made a deal and Nick put together a healthy program for her that Jenn *ignored* because she felt she wasn't losing fast enough. And for the record, Nick was beside himself when it happened. He wouldn't turn loose of her for a long time afterward because she'd given him such a fright."

Megan stared into the flames created by the gas logs, her thoughts her own. Finally she inhaled, and he knew she'd come to a conclusion when her body relaxed against his side.

"So, Nick's never given her a hard time about her appearance? You're sure?"

"Megan, Nick can't keep his hands off your sister. Trust me, he has no problem with her appearance. His love for her goes much deeper than that. Now I have a few questions for you. Who made you worry that Jenn was being abused? Not Mrs. Stouts—I know she's a gossip and you probably heard the story from her. I want to know who made you worry about it in the first place. Who gave you the nightmares that make you so jumpy? Who scared you?"

Megan lowered the spoon to her bowl and tried to smile, but the effort was weak and completely unbelievable. "Just because I'm wondering about it doesn't mean— Where are you going?"

He'd removed his arm from around her shoulders and sat forward on the couch, ready to stand. "I'd hoped you'd be honest with me. It's time, don't you think? Especially after what happened in the kitchen?"

A huff left her chest. "Oh, I get it. You talk to me about Nick and Jenn, but because I'm not gushing out my life story, you're going to go clean?" she asked, snorting. "You know you have a problem, don't you?"

"I'm not obsessive-compulsive."

"Yeah, and my ex-husband wasn't a jerk. He was a nightmare from start to finish, okay? But you—You want to know why you can't relate to Simon? I've figured it out if you're interested."

One look at her face had Ethan wanting to jump up and get out of there, but he forced himself to remain seated beside her. Why hadn't he just kept on kissing her? If he had, they'd be in bed right now doing something a lot more appealing than arguing. "Tell me." It was as much of an acknowledgment as he could muster under the circumstances.

"You're not going to like it."

Go figure. Who wanted to be roasted over hot coals?

"Look, I'm just going to say it, okay? Simon's reacting to the whole cleaning thing."

"What do you mean?"

"I mean, why so much?"

Trust was fragile, but he'd begun to build a level of trust with Megan. If he overreacted to her criticism, he could blow all the progress he'd made with her. *So don't overreact.* "Megan, I'm not O.C."

Megan's expression clearly stated that she was convinced otherwise. "It's been said before?"

"Garret," he admitted reluctantly. "He joked about it when he lived here, but I've always been neat." And that sounded way too defensive.

"Ethan." She placed her ice-cream-cold fingers on his arm. "Neatness is one thing, but have you always cleaned the kitchen cabinets at three in the morning?"

He studied her, noticing that since she'd arrived the shadows were gone from beneath her eyes, and she'd lost the stark, gaunt look from three steady meals a day. A wave of protectiveness washed over him, through him, and for a guy known for his two-to-screw dating system, the power behind the awareness terrified him.

He wasn't ready for this. He couldn't handle Simon, much less a relationship with a woman who was such a challenging mix of beauty, smart-mouthed sass and vulnerability. It brought out his possessive side even as it made him want to get up and run. He wanted to kiss her, take her to bed. Tell her to shut up, because he wasn't O.C. and that's obviously where the conversation was headed. And even though he knew she trembled at confronting him over what she believed to be his problem with Simon, she did it anyway, ratcheting up his admiration for her. "Megan, I can't sleep and it's how I keep busy. Wear myself down. I'm not O.C."

"Okay, fine. You're not. But it doesn't change the fact that Simon can't relax here."

Can't relax? What did that have to do with cleaning? "I'm not following."

She stroked his arm gently, distractedly. "At first I didn't pay any attention because I thought it was just his personality and he was withdrawn and quiet, but then…"

"Then what? What have you noticed?"

"I've *noticed* your constant cleaning, and needing everything to be put away before he's barely finished playing with it. It's freaking him out. To be honest, it's freaking me out, too," she added, looking away, "but it's really messing with Simon. I think he's afraid. When I spilled the flour…"

She closed her eyes and a look of heartache flashed over her face. Pain. She scooted forward to set her bowl on a magazine atop the coffee table and flashed him a look he couldn't quite interpret. The fire hissed behind the grate, the burning gas the only noise in the room other than the old-fashioned mantel clock ticking softly from its perch.

"After I made the mess, I was…upset. But then Simon got upset and I wanted to show him that it was okay, so we started playing in it and goofing off. Ethan, he laughed, *really* laughed. I've seen Simon smile, but the sound made me realize I haven't heard him laugh the entire time I've been here."

He hadn't, either. And he regretted that he hadn't been around to hear it.

"The two can't be coincidence. The flour was all over the place and things were a mess and for the first time Simon didn't look like he was ready to be punished for something. He relaxed and played and he had fun. But before, when we were in the kitchen and everything was all nice and tidy, I was trying to get him to help and he just sat there like always, like he was scared to touch anything and mess it up." She shot him a long glance from beneath her lashes. "That's why I think he's afraid of making a mess, afraid you'll be upset or disappointed, maybe even afraid he'll be punished or that you'll send him away."

A fist to his gut couldn't have been more surprising. The air left his lungs and he surged to his feet, crossing the room in three quick strides until he realized he had nowhere to go. "He thinks I'd send him back to Niger?"

Megan's eyes glittered in the firelight, a little wary, definitely sad, but soft and determined and brave.

"He never said that or indicated that. This is just my opinion, but—Ethan, he's *five*. What does a five-year-old really understand about adoption? And you clean so much, expect everything to be so freaking *neat* all the time, I think Simon equates him making a mess to being bad. He went to school in Niger, right? Ethan, Simon has manners and someone taught them very well. Think about it—when you're a guest in someone's house, aren't you supposed to be a little more conscious of what you're doing? Aren't you on your best behavior? Do you not mind your manners and—" her voice lowered "—behave so that you're asked back or allowed to stay?"

He stood there, stunned by her words and realizing they had merit. Was that really how Simon felt? What he believed? "I need some air."

"Ethan, wait."

"Good night, Megan."

Ethan scrubbed a hand over his face and headed for the back door, beyond tired, his mind racing. Angry at her words, angry at himself. Because it was true. He knew it was true.

But if he was such a basket case, how would he ever be the father Simon needed?

THE NEXT FEW DAYS were spent attempting to avoid Ethan. Why had Megan opened her mouth and accused him of being obsessive-compulsive? What business of hers was it if he cleaned his own house? It meant she had less to do, so she ought to be happy and leave the man alone.

But you didn't leave him alone, did you?

No, she'd kissed him. Responded to him and nearly screamed in frustration on his kitchen counter. Now she stood mere inches from where Ethan had made it to second base with her, alternately loading the dishwasher and glaring at the phone because it didn't ring. *Call me, Jenn. Just* talk *to me. You used to listen to my boy problems and try to give me advice. Well? I'm ready to listen now and you don't even care.*

Like Jenn would approve of her kissing Ethan? Megan sighed. She just knew Jenn would be able to take one look at her face and know she'd had her tongue in Ethan's mouth, so she hadn't even had the courage to take the cookies to Jenn's for another attempt to talk. There was the whole diet regime thing, too. She didn't want to sidetrack Jenn if she was trying to lose weight.

Instead she'd had Simon bag up the cookies and they'd taken them to the kids at story hour and swim class. Simon loved the water and liked to swim, and the cookies had been a hit with the kids, earning Simon some automatic friends.

A shiver of unease worked its way down her spine when she remembered the way an older, balding man had looked at her at the Y. She'd sat in the waiting area with the other adults and glanced up to see a man being escorted through the building by one of the workers. The worker was apparently giving the man a tour of the facility, but Megan's instincts had gone haywire until the two had moved on.

A *thump* startled her. Megan whirled to face the sound, realizing too late that it was merely Ethan's palm pushing open the swinging kitchen door. He noticed her reaction, though. His eyes narrowed shrewdly, and she turned her back on him and went back to what she was doing.

"I think we need to change Simon's bedtime. He's looking more tired than usual."

Megan leaned her head back on her neck and made a face, rolling her eyes. But when she straightened and lifted her lashes, she gasped when she saw Ethan watching her in the reflection of the window. Caught in the act, she didn't know what to say, what do to. So she simply ducked her head and waited for his reaction, gripping the plate until her fingers hurt.

Remember, anything can be a weapon. Do they play fair when they hit you? No. Is it fair that men are bigger and stronger? No. Use anything at your disposal to even the odds.

The self-defense instructor's voice appeared out of nowhere. A part of her said she could trust Ethan, a part of her wanted to trust him. But after the man at the Y had given her the creeps, a bigger part of her wanted to run, because what if she did trust Ethan and she was wrong again?

"What's the matter now? I played with Simon instead of doing the dishes. I thought that would've earned points with you."

Earned points? Apparently she and Simon weren't the only ones in moods tonight. Simon had been grumpy and cranky all day, easily moved to tears as they drove from one place to another and attended story hour, swimming and orientation at karate. But add in food breaks, schooling and bath time and the child had kicked up a fuss because he wanted to watch television and it was time to go to bed so he could do it all over again tomorrow.

Ethan walked to the fridge to get something to drink and Megan glanced over her shoulder, noting the way tension creased the side of Ethan's mouth. His shoulders were lined and tight, almost drawn up to his ears.

"Stop watching me like I'm a snake about to strike. Whatever it is, just spit it out."

Her grip tightened on the plate and, even though she ordered herself to keep her mouth shut, she said, "Not when you're using that kind of tone."

The words hung in the thick air, and she could feel Ethan's stare boring a hole into her back. Head down, she glanced at their reflection in the window, waiting, ready to make a run for it if she had to.

Seconds passed. Ethan lifted his hand and wiped it over his face, rubbing his mouth and chin. Breath by breath his shoulders lowered. "Sorry. You're right. I'm in a lousy mood and I'm taking it out on you. I just can't seem to do anything right with the kid."

She didn't move, not yet. "Ethan, Simon's tired. Just cut him some slack. Maybe you're trying too hard."

A soft curse filled the air. "I'm trying too hard, I'm cleaning too much."

Did she always have to stick her foot in her mouth? "You know what I meant."

"I do," he said after a few seconds passed. "You rolled your eyes when I mentioned Simon's bedtime. Why?"

Sensing he was on a more even keel, she put the plate and the last of the utensils in the dishwasher, tossed in a detergent square and shut the door. "No reason. I'm tired, too. I think I'll go to bed early tonight."

He stepped in front of her and blocked the exit. "We're going to talk about this."

Megan stiffened, and after the day's events, her thoughts slid back to another time, another place. Another man. *"You think you're going somewhere, bitch?"*

She flinched at the memory and backed up a step, realizing too late that step placed her in a corner. "Not now. Get out of my way."

"Megan, sweetheart, come on. I'm sorry for snapping at you earlier. Things have been tense and it's my fault. I didn't like hearing you say I have a problem, but you're entitled to your opinion. Let's just drop it and move on, shall we?"

She focused on Ethan's chin, trying desperately to shove the memories away. Ethan had been tense, upset, angry and passionate—and not once had he ever raised his hand or voice to her or Simon. Ethan could've taken advantage of her and had sex that night instead of stopping. He wasn't Sean. But as she'd discovered, old memories never truly died and tonight hers were out in full force. "I just want t-to go to bed."

"Not yet."

"Sean, please, I just want to go to bed."

"Not yet, you're not. You think you know everything, don't you? You think I don't see those faces you make behind my back? Eh?"

"I'm sorry—Ow! Ow!"

Megan turned and gripped the curved edge of the countertop, unable to breathe. What was wrong with her? The man today hadn't been watching her, he hadn't been any more interested in her than he'd been in any of the other women there. Sean might have been released from prison, but he wasn't following her. He wasn't—

Ethan's hands settled on her shoulders and she jumped.

"Shh. Hey, take it easy. Take a breath. Come on, deep breath. That's it."

The soothing, crooning sound of Ethan's voice broke through the terror of the memories engulfing her, dragging her down, under. Stiff, she let Ethan pull her back against his chest, let him hold her, his lips in her hair as he murmured nonsense. But unlike his words, everything wasn't okay. She wasn't okay. Would she ever feel normal again? Be comfortable with a man and not worry about the size of his fists? The anger in his tone?

"Come on. I've got the baby monitor. Let's go outside and get some air." Ethan kept one arm around her as he snagged their jackets from the hooks by the door. They paused on the deck to shrug them on, then Ethan took her hand in his, holding it loosely while they meandered off the deck into the yard, over to the picnic table under the big maple that held the tree house. The fallen leaves crunched under their feet as they neared the tree, and Ethan seated himself atop the table and pulled her between his legs, snuggling her close once again.

"You going to tell me what that was about?"

Megan knew she should protest the familiarity. Kissing Ethan had been a mistake. He was her boss and she needed this job and he was right. Every kiss, every touch. They couldn't go back and pretend they hadn't happened. But Ethan's hands warmed her, made her burn with a different kind of need, and right now she needed something to ground her, something to keep her from flying off into the fear, the darkness of her memories.

"Megan?"

She needed a new memory, something to erase Sean's

touch, and in her heart of hearts she knew Ethan was the man to show her, teach her, what intimacy was all about. "Ethan?"

"What, sweetheart?"

"Kiss me."

Chapter 17

HE DIDN'T HAVE to be told twice. With the press of his lips, the taste of his tongue, Ethan's kiss rocked her to her core. How much of her life had been wasted on losers? Her loser boyfriend in high school who'd only wanted to get laid by the head cheerleader. The loser in college who dumped her for a girl willing to have a threesome. Sean.

With a whimper she wrapped her arms around Ethan's neck and gave herself over to him. He deepened the kiss, but when he made no move to do more than kiss, she shifted out of his arms and headed for the tree house.

"Megan?"

The hoarse sound of her name on his lips set her body on fire. But what else could she expect? She was playing with fire. Her job, her future. But she was a doer and for once in her life she was going to *do* and have no regrets. Ethan wasn't a loser. He was caring and kind, sexy and good.

Ethan followed her up the ladder into the tree house. Once inside, he framed her face in his hands and groaned when she rubbed her body against him. She could feel his arousal growing hard and thick against her stomach, knew exactly where this was going to lead and wanted more. So much more.

HIS HANDS SLID beneath her jacket and shirt. The cool roughness of his fingers against her skin sent shivers up her spine but this time the trembling inside her wasn't the result of fear but pure desire, especially when he slipped his hands up until he unfastened her bra and cupped her breasts in his hands.

"Mmm, you're warm."

He whispered the words against her neck, tried to kiss her again, but she dislodged his hands and pulled away again, grabbing the sleeping bag from the corner where she and Simon had left it, and spread it out on the tree house floor.

"Megan, are you sure?"

More sure of this than of anything she'd done in the past. This time she wasn't a hormonal teenager out to prove her sexual power, she wasn't a college freshman trying to stay popular. She wasn't her sister's protector or Sean's punching bag. She was a woman, stronger, wiser, determined to leave the past behind by sharing her body with a man she cared for way too much.

How could she resist him? Ethan's gaze was glittering and hot, humble. He wanted her, she could tell, but he was willing to go back to the house as though he wasn't turned on and aching. That awareness, that knowledge, made her want him all the more; he was so tender she knew she was safe.

His eyes locked on hers, Ethan knelt and pulled off her boots, one at a time, leaving her socks on for comfort on the cold wood floor. Her jeans were next and he fussed over the goose bumps that came when he tugged the denim down her legs, kissing the skin he revealed to the cold.

Ethan went to work on his clothes next, toeing off his shoes and shucking his pants and underwear before joining her in the single-person bag. It was a tight fit but that just brought them closer. The cold disappeared with the heat of his body, and the rasp of his hairy legs against hers made her smile as she curled her arms around his neck and pulled his head low.

One kiss turned into three before Ethan broke contact and explored her body with a passion unlike any she'd ever experienced. He seemed intent and entirely focused on bringing her pleasure, driving her insane with little nips and kisses and bites that sent her pulse roaring through her ears. Tender-rough hands slid under her shirt once more, lifting it up so he could kiss and caress her breasts.

"Beautiful."

"I'm too small."

"More than a handful is wasted."

She almost laughed at the old line, but she didn't, couldn't. Not when by simply saying the words, Ethan accepted her just as she was. He made her feel beautiful, not something to be possessed or owned, not a trophy to show off to the world. Ethan appreciated her body, and she loved how he looked at her, as if he held nothing back. His eyes burned hot, only for her, and the way he touched her, made love to her—

No, sex, not love. Don't confuse the two.

A small whimper filled the air as she forced the thoughts away. His fingers tangled in her hair, his palm cradling her head tenderly as he claimed her mouth and held her in place while he made her forget everything but the feel of his arms.

Her hands curled over the steely strength of his biceps, up his back. Hard muscle, velvet skin. How was it possible to feel so different? To be so strong yet gentle?

Ethan's hand trailed low, and he lifted her leg, teasing her inner thigh with a stroke of his fingers that left her gasping, wanting. Closer and closer but never quite there. The tantalizing strokes made her arch and squirm, holding her breath because she wanted him to fill the ache inside her.

Ethan was so in tune to what made her body hum. Her responses visibly turned him on, and she liked knowing he cared enough to want her with him.

The urgency built. Kisses became longer, breathing rougher. Murmured words of beauty and praise and all the things they were going to do before the night was over. Her hands smoothed over his ribs, lower, until she made him groan and drop his forehead to her collarbone, his breath hot and moist on her skin. The moment seared itself in her mind, the smell and taste of him, the cool night air, the quietness of the tree house and the way she felt so safe.

"My pants. Wait a second."

She felt bereft when Ethan pulled away and rustled through his pants pocket for protection. She couldn't stop touching him, stroking his back while he fumbled to don the condom, stroking his stomach and smiling when he growled at her because his body jumped in response.

"You'll pay for that."

The words gave her pause for a moment, until her mind kicked in and she realized her body wasn't scared. If anything, the tenderly voiced threat turned her on with all the potential ways he could see it through. "Promises, promises."

Protection in place, Ethan dropped his head for a heady, soul-deep kiss, and she savored the feel of his tongue in her mouth, the rough scrub of his cheeks against her chin. So good. Why had she waited this long?

With a teasing smile he sucked at the sensitive skin of her shoulder and neck, and slipped his hand low to tease and test her readiness. Sensation swept through her when he found just the right spot and stroked. She shut her eyes with a moan.

Finally Ethan settled himself over her. "You with me, sweetheart?"

Her breath caught in her throat when he nudged her, barely making contact. Any more with him and she was going to implode. "Bring it on already."

A husky chuckle left him at her order. Ethan's smiling lips covered hers and muffled her moan of absolute welcome when he slid home. There was a sense of pressure, fullness, the toe-curling heat that made her lift her knees and tilt her hips so he'd touch just the right way. So good. So, *so* good.

Everything faded as his hips began pumping into her, the confines of the sleeping bag grinding him against her and making her squirm. Faster, deeper. Perfect strokes that drove the tension inside her higher.

Megan held on, reveling in the moment. Taking all of him, wanting more, her body growing tighter with every grinding lunge. "Eth—"

He smothered her cry with his lips, his body moving over hers, in hers, as the world swirled around her and she climaxed. Ethan's hoarse groan filled her ears as he found his own release, and she held him close, her heart hurting because she knew—she *knew*—she'd never be the same again.

THANKSGIVING at the Tulane family home was an
event to behold. Family members from four states made
the drive, and everyone had made it home except for
Ethan's baby sister. Alexandra was somewhere in the wilds
of Alaska, stuck there due to a snowstorm, but a whispered
comment between his sisters-in-law had him wondering if
there wasn't some guy to blame for her absence. It
wouldn't do for her to get too attached. Alaska was too
damn far away. Besides, what was it they said about the
men there? The odds are good but the goods are odd?

Movement from the corner of the room drew his attention, and Ethan found himself unable to take his eyes off
Megan, or keep his thoughts from drifting to what was
beneath the dark brown wrap dress she wore. The way the
dress clung to her curves he knew she wore one of the
thongs he favored.

The past week had been nothing like any in his experience. They shared breakfast in the morning, then he went
off to work. He arrived home in time to share Simon's
bedtime ritual, waiting for the boy to fall asleep before
Ethan and Megan tore at each other's clothes and lost
themselves to the chemistry that burned so hot.

Megan was playing things cool, quite a switch from his
previous bed partners' attempts to land a ring on their
finger. Not Megan. She avoided his hints to talk more
about her past and what their future held, pretended it was
just sex. But she was wrong.

She knew it, he knew it, but she wasn't ready to admit
it yet. And that was fine with him. For now. He wasn't quite
sure how to react to the situation himself since, until now,
he'd never found himself contemplating more than a
casual affair.

Having played the field since his teens, he knew his
fascination with Megan was more than a passing fancy. But

with her focus on making amends with Jenn and his on getting appointed chief, where did that leave them? Better yet, where did that leave Simon?

Every day Ethan fell more and more behind at work, but a part of him didn't care because he was growing so frustrated at the time he was required to spend away from his family.

His family. He liked the sound of that.

"So have you heard any news from the board?" His father seated himself on the stool and grabbed the remote control from the table, turning up the sound to be heard over the cracking of billiard balls. The game room in the basement of his parents' house was filled with his male cousins and brothers, everyone hanging out and waiting to be called to the table.

"Not yet." He inhaled and sighed, his thoughts shifting to all the work that awaited him both on his dining room table at home and his desk at the hospital. It had been one thing to sit and shift piles of paper when his leg was still healing and he couldn't stand for the required hours, but it was another thing to be well and able to perform surgery but not have the time due to the administrative requirements of the job.

His father's gaze narrowed, an astute frown bringing his bushy eyebrows low over his forehead. "Megan and Simon seem to be doing well together."

"They are. Megan's worked wonders with him. Simon's speaking more English every day."

"I heard." A pregnant pause filled the air. "Makes a pretty picture. The boy clings to her like she's his mama. Strange that he doesn't seem to do that as much with you."

"Direct hit." A make-believe explosion filled the air from the electronic Battleship game his young cousins played on the floor nearby.

The irony wasn't lost on Ethan. "We're still adjusting."

"A child needs his father." Alan channel surfed, changing the station from a recap of the Macy's parade to the lead-up to a bowl game. "Your mother and I are taking another cruise soon. I've decided to take that early retirement I've been talking about for so long. Just going to do it rather than drag it out forever. The cruise is to celebrate. We've always wanted to travel and we're not getting any younger."

"Mom will like that."

His father nodded his agreement. "Finally making the decision got me to thinking about all the things I missed when you kids were growing up."

And here we go. "I didn't mean to miss the game, Dad. Something came up and I couldn't leave. Besides, I've taken Simon off the roster for the season. I had him signed up for too much."

"Figured that out, did you?"

A flush crept up his neck. "Megan pointed it out." That, and a lot more. But he'd opened himself up to what she'd told him and was attempting to repair the damage. "Guess a part of me was trying to help Simon forget everything he's been through by keeping him too busy to think."

"I'm glad you figured out it doesn't work that way. But back to the game. I never meant to miss the games or plays or events, either, but I did. Sometimes it can't be helped, and it's the price we pay to do what we do. But you need to know it's not the same, viewing everything through pictures and video after the fact. Just mentioning it, in case you might want to rethink taking on more responsibility."

Rethink it? "You mean being chief?"

His father lifted a hand to where Simon and Matt played in the far corner. A pile of Lincoln Logs was scattered on the floor between them.

"That goes by much too fast. I'm ashamed to say I barely remember you at that age because I was home so rarely. It's one of my biggest regrets."

One he had no intention of making with Simon. He just had to figure out a way of juggling it all.

That'll require more than day care or a nanny.

Ethan frowned at the thought, but it was true. And who better to help him at home than a wife?

His gaze immediately shifted to Megan. After introducing her to everyone, she'd accompanied Simon to the basement to play, hovering over him more than normal, and obviously nervous over being there, given her situation with Jenn.

His gaze narrowed. Life with Megan would be chaos and mess and sassy comebacks. Great sex. Constant tension, because she and Jenn didn't get along. Tenderness.

"Just something to think about. When the time comes, I'm sure you'll make the right decision for everyone."

Ah, but there was the kicker—what was the right decision? Megan trusted him up to a point, but not completely. The job he wanted and had worked his whole career to get meant longer hours and little family time. And Simon… The boy was doing better but they still had a long way to go before they were comfortable together, as his father had pointed out.

How did he know the right decision to make when he couldn't see the forest for the trees?

The pager on his belt went off first, then his cell phone began to ring. Ethan winced when he spotted the number and code on the face. Damn. Another holiday biting the dust.

"Drive safe, son. And don't forget about what I said."

"I will, if you don't let Garret eat all the turkey."

Chapter 18

JENN SET THE BOX she carried on the sofa table and pulled off the lid, but the moment she saw Megan enter the room she made a face. "Shouldn't you be watching Simon?"

Megan was in the mood for a fight so she planted herself in front of the exit. "He's fine."

"I don't need the stress right now, okay, Megs?"

Megan looked closely at Jenn's face, noting her extreme paleness. "Something wrong?"

Jenn tossed the box lid aside. "Yeah, you're here. And you keep calling my house."

"Return my calls and I'll stop. I'm not after your husband," she said, careful that her voice didn't carry to the other room. Not that anyone would venture into the sunroom with her and Jenn inside it.

"Thank God for small favors. However, since you are obviously sleeping with Ethan, you're up to your old tricks. You don't ever think of anyone but yourself, do you?"

Hurt lanced deep. When they'd first arrived she'd made a point to avoid close contact with Ethan in an attempt at discretion. But after Ethan's return from the hospital, he'd followed her around like a guilty puppy and for good reason. Some hospital emergency. Since when did bringing a beautiful woman home to his parents' house for Thanksgiving qualify as an emergency?

"Why are you letting a very young, very *traumatized* little boy get attached to you? It's not fair to him. How *dare* you."

Forced into the moment, she sighed. She'd thought of that, worried about it, but had hoped things would work out for the best. At the very least she'd figured things would be okay until whatever was between her and Ethan had run its course.

What an idiot she'd been for thinking she and Ethan would last longer than a week. *He brought another woman. Another woman!*

You can't complain. You're the one who made a big deal about keeping things casual. In guy-speak that means Ethan is free to do as he pleases.

But it pissed her off. What kind of arrogant jerk would bring *two* women to Thanksgiving dinner? What, was he starting a harem? "I wouldn't hurt Simon for anything." Ethan on the other hand...

"You will hurt him. The longer you stay, the worse it will be. And what about Ethan? Megan, he's your boss."

She pictured the exotic-looking woman in the other room. If Ethan's gesture didn't serve to tell Megan exactly where she stood in his life, nothing would. Such a jerk!

She tried and failed to ignore the flood of pain pouring through her. She wanted to leave but didn't have a way off the mountaintop home short of stealing a car. That wasn't out of the realm of possibility at this point, but if Jenn had her way, the cops would be called and Megan wasn't going to jail over a stupid man. "Stop worrying. Ethan will no doubt marry someone like her," she said with what she hoped was a breezy, uncaring, screw-him—oh, wait, I already did—wave of her hand toward the door. "They'll be nice and boring and—and *neat* together."

"Oh, I don't know about that, dear." Ethan's grandmother, Rosetta, entered the room, carrying another ornament box. Dressed all in black with sparkly earrings and a splashy wrap in pumpkin-orange silk, she looked classy and beautiful.

Like Dr. Portia Lucca. What kind of name was Portia, anyway? It was a freaking car.

"I do believe Dr. Lucca is all alone for the holiday. I'm sure that's why Ethan invited her to join us. I don't believe there is anything going on between them."

She didn't care. She really didn't. It wasn't like they could have a real relationship, anyway, not unless she came clean and finally told him the truth about Sean. But why put herself through the humiliation when Ethan had obviously already grown bored? He might be able to fool his Grammi but he wasn't fooling her!

A smile formed on Rosetta's lips, the color a deeper, richer pumpkin than her wrap. "As to whom Ethan will marry, I personally think he's drawn to someone more... lively. As well he should be. He needs someone who'll loosen him up a bit, especially now that he has Simon to care for. They both returned from Niger very much in need of someone who cares for them and understands them, someone fun." Rosetta handed the box to Jenn. "And wouldn't it be wonderful if Ethan could find love like you and Nick? Someone who makes him and Simon both smile?"

Her sister paled even more, her bottom lip quivering. "It would be nice, but it would be a mistake if you're considering Megan."

"Jenn." It was a whispered plea for her sister not to air her sordid past to Ethan's grandmother. At least not now. Besides, Rosetta couldn't have meant her.

Rosetta gave her a friendly smile. "Don't be afraid, dear. Just believe. Things work out in ways you least expect them to if you have faith. Plans have been known to change." Rosetta faced Jenn once more and patted Jenn's hand where she held the box. "People change. We need to remember that. Now, girls, it's Thanksgiving, a time of peace, harmony and forgiveness. I do believe you both have a lot to be thankful for, and it's time for you two to stop acting like children and get along."

Neither of them responded.

Megan stared at Jenn, wishing for the impossible. Jenn, Ethan, Simon. Today wasn't her day to be thankful, because everything she ever wanted was slipping through her fingers.

Rosetta sighed. "Megan, would you help me sort through some of the ornaments while we wait on the turkey to finish cooking?"

ETHAN WATCHED as Megan and Gram walked away and noted Jenn blinked away tears. "For what it's worth, I think she's sincere."

Jenn froze in the act of getting an ornament out of the box. Ethan walked deeper into the room but she ignored him. Several of the ornaments were in need of hooks, and she busied herself by finding them, blinking rapidly all the while. He gave her time to compose herself by moving to the box and plucking the ornaments out of the sectioned cardboard, handing them to her silently. "Do you really hate her so much?"

She sniffled. "I don't like her and I don't trust her. If you cared for someone and found out Nick betrayed you, you'd feel the same way."

"I guess I would. It does take a pretty nasty person to do what she did to you."

"She's not nasty, she's just…immature."

"So you do hate her."

"I love Meg—" She broke off and turned to him, catching on to his game. "Mind your own business."

"Tell me why you can't forgive her."

"I have."

"Then what's the problem? Come on, do you really think she's after Nick? Surely you know better than that."

She lifted her chin to a haughty angle. "Nick would have nothing to do with her—and she's sleeping with you."

"So you're keeping her at a distance because…?"

This time no amount of blinking could keep the tears at bay, and they trickled over her cheeks, making him hope Nick didn't come into the room and pummel him for making Jenn cry.

"Because…maybe because I don't want to find out if she'd do it again. It's easier this way."

So Jenn still had her doubts. "Easier, huh?" Ethan pulled her into a one-armed hug. "Easier wouldn't leave you crying. You're already hurting. Maybe if you listened to her side of things. Just saying," he said when she stiffened, "maybe you'd realize of the two of you, your big sister is the weaker one."

She snorted. "Not likely. Ethan, that statement proves that she's snowed you. She's trouble and you're falling for it."

"Spunk and attitude can hide a lot of fear." He wiped away a tear with his fingertip. "So can pride. Haven't you ever wondered what she's trying so hard to hide?"

MEGAN FOLLOWED Ethan into the house, her arms full of leftovers, her mind full of doubts and fears, a boatload of anger and way too many insecurities. Lord have mercy, what a day.

After Rosetta's order to get along, Jenn had reluctantly made an effort and while the conversation didn't exactly flow, when the others entered the room to decorate the family tree, she and Jenn had managed to stand next to each other without running for cover.

As to Ethan and his date—

"Don't move. I'll put Simon to bed and then we need to talk."

A shiver of want went through her at the look on his face and, even though she told herself to ignore him and go to bed—locking the door, of course—the rebel in her who'd taken Rosetta's words to heart wouldn't let her good-girl wannabe run. He owed her an explanation and running meant taking the easy way out. Either she wanted to take a chance with Ethan or not. Was she interested in him? In staying?

Megan made her way into the kitchen without turning on the light and piled the containers into the fridge, wondering how this house had become home so fast.

The truth had hit her tonight when she'd sat across the dinner table from Ethan and Simon and watched them interact. The wave of possession that had swept over her had taken her breath and made her want to scratch Portia's eyes out. Simon and Ethan were hers. They'd burrowed into her heart and taken root, healed the broken pieces of her soul and made her want and dream of so much more. But that meant she had to fight for what she wanted. Was she ready to do that?

One thing's for sure, you're tired of running.

But who knew what Ethan felt?

You haven't given him a chance to tell you. You've shut him down every time he's tried to get close.

And then he'd appeared with Dr. Lucca. She *had* sat at the opposite end of the table talking with Alan and Marilyn Tulane during dinner, and Ethan hadn't seemed to mind. In fact, he'd seemed relieved. But what did that mean? Ugh, why were men so confusing!

But even if—and it was a big *if*—Ethan wasn't interested in the gorgeous doctor, where did it leave her? Staying meant taking a chance. She'd just have to hope that when Ethan learned what she'd put up with, allowed Sean to do by living as his wife for years, Ethan would want her anyway.

And if not?

Simon's finger-painted pictures and coloring book pages were displayed on the refrigerator door—something Ethan had managed to ignore, even though she knew it killed him that it looked so messy. But the manic cleaning at three o'clock in the morning had stopped—partly because she liked to distract him with other things, and because she loved making love to him and helping him forget Niger and all that had happened.

Megan lifted her hand and traced her fingers over the globs of dried paint on Simon's handprint turkey, each of his fingers a different color. Beside that was a crayon drawing of the three of them. Ethan and Simon and her, just like a family.

The knot that formed in her stomach cut off her air supply. *Like a real family.* Was Jenn right? With her future so undecided, was it fair of her to let Simon get close?

Don't be afraid, just believe.

Rosetta's words sounded in her head, repeating several

times. Megan shook them away. Ethan had brought someone else to the dinner. A *date*. She could ignore the cleaning to some extent, she could ignore a lot of things, but she couldn't ignore that.

He didn't drive her home. Garret and Darcy drove her home since they were headed in that direction.

Oh, get over yourself already. That doesn't mean Portia isn't interested in Ethan—or him in her. They could be doin' it in the on-call rooms.

You either trust him or you don't.

And wasn't it all about trust?

"Shut up, shut up. You're going in circles. Just confront him. What's he going to do?" She laid her forehead against the cool refrigerator. "Beat you?" she whispered under her breath. "Been there, done that."

"Do you always talk to yourself?"

Megan whipped around at the sound of Ethan's voice. Had he heard her?

Knees weak, she leaned against the fridge, taking in Ethan's casual dress—khaki pants and a long-sleeved shirt—his rugged, seriously handsome face.

Some men were violent. Not Ethan. No, he'd never hurt her or Simon, and if she wanted Ethan, she had to be a grown-up and voice her thoughts and fears and give him the chance to refute them. If she wanted this chance, she had to take it, not push it away.

"Megan, I want you to listen to me and listen good. Portia was *not* a date."

"I know. She was alone at the hospital, so you invited her for dinner." She nodded her understanding, sarcastic though it was.

"Exactly. If she were a date, I would've taken her home."

"Maybe."

"No, not maybe. She wasn't a date—" he hesitated slightly "—but I'd be lying if I said we were no more than colleagues."

Just when you thought it was safe to go back into the water. What the heck did that mean? That he had slept with her?

"Megan, Portia is my therapist." He lifted a shoulder in an uncomfortable shrug. "After you and I talked about the cleaning issue and Simon being uncomfortable, I went to talk to Portia about Simon and…wound up talking about me. I'd rather you not say anything to anyone, especially my family."

His therapist? Relief poured through her. "Of course not." He was embarrassed. She'd seen Ethan's progress recently. There had been times when she could tell he'd wanted to pick things up and put them away. She had to acknowledge that Ethan was better. He didn't seem to get as stressed when he saw the construction paper strewn about or the plates piled in the sink ready to be loaded into the dishwasher. And to have actually gone to see a therapist? He'd *listened* to her, admitted his problem and was trying to work on it. She didn't know what to say.

"She has a fiancé," he added quickly. "In Boston. He's moving here in a few months and they're getting married this spring."

Smiling, Megan moved to him, her body growing achy, tingling, empty inside. "Good for her. And thank you for telling me. For trusting me enough to tell me." She lifted her hands to his arms, slid them up his chest, around his neck. Ethan was solid and warm, musk and spice. Strength and comfort. She should have trusted he wouldn't betray her that way.

Well, she trusted him now. And she'd tell him everything. Soon. She didn't want him to look at her and see the suspicious, distrusting woman Sean had beaten. She wanted Ethan to see the woman she'd become, stronger. Forgiving. "I, um, want to talk to you, too. I want to tell you some things about me and my marriage, but—" she wet her lips and saw his gaze drop to her mouth "—I don't want to do it right now. I'm in the mood for something else."

His hands fell to her hips, and his palms smoothed over the thin material of the dress. Megan smiled at the way his eyes darkened the moment he traced the scraps of material at her hip bones. Ethan liked her lingerie skimpy and sleek.

"And what would that be?"

She glanced around, spotted the counter located next to the swing door and decided right then she wanted to rock Ethan's world. Simon was asleep. The boy hadn't had any nightmares for almost two weeks, and if he did wake up and come look for them, he'd try to push the door inward. But if something blocked it…

Megan grasped Ethan's hand and led him to the counter. Once there she flashed Ethan what she hoped was a seductive glance from beneath her lashes and lifted herself up onto the counter as he had that night weeks ago. Ethan moved between her parted legs in an instant, his hands slipping beneath the hem of her dress, bunching the material and holding her gaze as he oh, so slowly trailed his fingers up her thighs to find the straps of her underwear. He pulled them out of the way.

"You won't be needing these."

In the quiet house all that could be heard was the quickened rasp of their breathing, the sounds of belts and zips. They kissed long and deep, stifled moans when caresses brought them too close to the edge of fulfillment. The height of the counter brought her to eye level with Ethan and when he finally removed a condom from his wallet, because they'd learned to make the most of their opportunities when Simon was asleep, Megan's hands dropped, caressing the length of him.

"Sweet—*Megan.*"

Sealing his mouth over hers, Ethan nudged her hands away and positioned himself, slid home and began moving inside her in a slow, tantalizing pace. Hard met soft, teased, heat expanded and swelled and made her tighten and try to hold on to him, because as Ethan filled her, he made her whole again. Made her dream.

Made her believe.

Chapter 19

IT WAS BOYS' NIGHT IN at the Y. Ethan had taken Simon to watch a showing of *Finding Nemo*, which meant Megan had the perfect opportunity to talk to Jenn and settle things once and for all about the past as well as Megan's relationship with Ethan. And if Jenn refused to open the door?

That's what Grandma Lucy's recipe cards and Jenn's autographed copy of Nancy Drew are for.

Shameless, shameless, shameless.

Megan took a deep breath and stared at Jenn's front door, Rosetta's words in her head. She had to believe that Jenn would forgive her. Had to. Believe it, see it, make it happen. Nodding to herself like a bobblehead, Megan knocked three times in rapid succession.

Jenn opened the door with a yank. "It's about—" Her expression crumpled. "You've got to be kidding me." Jenn rolled her eyes toward the sky above. *"Now?"*

"Can I come in?"

"Why? What are you doing here?"

Megan took another deep breath and brought Jenn's

attention to the items in her hands. "Here. These are for you. I'm sorry about the doll. I'll see if I can't find another one like it." There. Done. Dammit, would she just take the stuff?

"Grandma's recipes?"

"Just so you know, I copied them—but the originals are all here. And your book—see? I kept it safe. I'm sorry I took it." Megan shoved the items toward Jenn then tucked her hands into the pockets of the coat Ethan had purchased for her.

"I can't believe you. You *took* them? Why?"

"Because I was jealous of you. Look, that doesn't matter now. I really want to make peace." She paused, then said, "It's, um, kind of cold out here. Can I come in?"

The phone rang. Two seconds later a timer went off in the back of the house where the kitchen was located.

Without a word Jenn whirled on her bare feet and hurried down the hall, and since Jenn hadn't told Megan she couldn't come in, Megan stepped over the threshold and shut the door behind her.

Yum. The smell of something wonderful filled the air and led the way to the kitchen.

"Hello?" Jenn held a portable between her head and shoulder and grabbed a pot holder, opening the oven door. "Suzanne, where *are* you? I thought you were at the door just now but—"

Jenn spotted Megan and broke off, lifting a hand and waving Megan away from inspecting the pots atop the stove. As always, Megan ignored the request and checked out the contents. Ribs, twice-baked potatoes—way too light on the butter—an assortment of veggies and, whoa, even Martha couldn't decorate a cake as pretty as that.

Lifting her gaze, she noticed the kitchen table was set

with crystal and candles and their mother's best china. When had Mom given Jenn those?

It doesn't matter. It's just a thing. Surprisingly, the pangs of jealousy she'd proclaimed as her excuse for lifting the book and recipes weren't there. Besides, any mother who'd blame the child for the father's sins…Why would Megan want a part of that history? Give her a chipped mug any day.

"Suzanne, you promised! You said you'd come over and do my hair and makeup and listen to me freak out because—"

Once again Megan felt Jenn's eyes on her when she broke off, turning her back to Megan.

Freak out about what? Obviously it was about something other than her presence in town since the table was set for a celebration—or a seduction. Oooh, Thumper planned on getting busy tonight, eh?

"No, I understand. Of course. I hope the baby gets feeling better soon. I will…Thanks. I'll let you know what he says. I hope so. I know he does but—Never mind. I'll talk to you later. Bye."

Jenn pressed the button on the phone and lifted both hands, phone included, to her head, pressing hard.

"Can I help?"

Jenn shook her head.

"Hey, all those years in pageants need to be used for good. And it looks like you've got something nice planned," Megan said, indicating the table. "I can have you done in half an hour, less if you hold still and I don't have to sit on you like the last time."

Jenn lowered the phone. "Megan, *why* are you here?"

"You want to talk or you want to get ready for tonight?"

Jenn took a deep breath, her expression wary. "Nick will be home in forty-five minutes."

"Where's your makeup?"

MEGAN BIT BACK a sarcastic grin as she watched Jenn try to prepare herself. Half an hour. She had Jenn's undivided attention for half an hour. *Please, God, don't let me screw this up.*

Megan dumped the makeup bag on the counter and dug in. It reminded her of when they were kids and how they'd play dress up—until Megan had to dress up for so many events and doing so made the novelty wear off. After that, anytime Jenn had asked to play, she'd scoffed and called her a baby—or sat on her, painted her face and took Polaroid pictures for blackmail purposes.

You know, you really could've been nicer.

"Don't use too much."

"I won't."

"I don't want to look like a slut."

Megan's hand paused ever so slightly as she dabbed foundation around Jenn's nose.

"You know what I mean. I don't like too much."

"I know. You're lucky because you never had to wear a lot in order to look good. You've got great skin. I've always been jealous of your skin."

"Yeah, right."

Okay, enough. "Can't you ever take a compliment? Seriously, Jenn, look at you. You're glowing." She nudged Jenn's shoulder. "The sex must be great."

"Megan."

Megan grabbed a brush and eye shadow next. "What are you wearing?"

Jenn bit her lip and waved her hand toward a dress hanging on the closet door, looking as though she waited for Megan to rip it to shreds. It was a silvery-gray that matched Jenn's eyes. "Great choice." She set the eye shadow down and went foraging again. "Here we go. Perfect. This one is different from the others. Impulse buy?"

"That's—A friend suggested it. You'd like Suzanne."

"Maybe I can meet her sometime."

Jenn moved to see herself in the mirror. "Hurry. My hair is a mess. Yours looks good, by the way. You colored it again."

"My roots were showing. And I know a great trick for making your hair look sexy and sophisticated. We've got plenty of time." But time was running out and they hadn't talked about anything serious. She cleared her throat. "Jenn…"

"I've always envied that about you," Jenn said softly. "You make all this girl stuff look easy."

"The girl stuff just takes practice."

"What about how you stay so thin? Is that practice?"

Eyeliner and mascara were next, lipstick. Then Megan started on Jenn's hair.

"Nope, that's stress, which isn't the way to do it. I might be thin but I don't look half as nice as you. You've always had a great shape. Don't roll your eyes, I mean it."

"You're piling on the compliments a little thick, Megs."

"Oh, yeah? Look at this." Megan turned and wiggled her butt, her pants sagging where her butt should've been. "And look at yours. You've never once had to pad your bra or your butt, have you?"

"You did not pad your butt," Jenn said, aghast but smiling.

"Ever see those things in the back of those cheesy

tabloids? I had them in three colors. I wore one under every evening gown to fill it out and give it an extra twitch when I walked."

"It just sounds so silly when being thin is what every woman wants."

"Is it?" Megan went back to work on Jenn's hair.

"It's all I've wanted for the last year but now…" The tears came out of nowhere and with a shaky breath she buried her face in her hands.

"No, the mascara's not—Oh, Jenn." Panic surged. Was Ethan wrong? "Jenn, don't cry. I'll help you, whatever it is. Tell me what to do."

"You can't do anything and I can't stop! H-how can something good be so horrible?"

"What? What's horrible?"

Jenn shook all over, tears flowing. "I'm so scared. I'm going to gain it all back. I just know I am." Jenn lifted her gaze and looked at Megan. "I'm going to be big and fat and everybody's going to talk about how thin you are and how much bigger I am. *How* do you do it? I've always hated you for always being skinny."

The words cut, even though Megan knew Jenn said them in frustration. She went back to work on Jenn's hair until she thought of a response, leaving the mascara mess for last since Jenn wasn't through crying yet. "If it helps, I always hated it that you were considered the smart one. No one ever seemed to consider that I might have been smart, too."

Jenn sniffled and grabbed one of Megan's hands. "I'm sorry. I didn't mean what I said. I truly don't hate you, I don't *hate* anyone, I've just always…wanted to be you."

Megan tilted her head to one side. "Irony's a pain, you know that? Weird how everybody wants what everyone else has, huh?"

Jenn wiped at her eyes and spotted a black smear. "Oh, no. I ruined it!"

"Stop. You'll make it worse. I'll fix it when I'm done with your hair and it'll be good as new." Megan dropped one long lock and grabbed another. "Since we're trading envy stories, I guess I could admit that I stole your nose."

"What?"

"Remember the nose job I got for my sweet sixteen? I wanted a car, but Dad bought me a nose instead. Way to go boosting the old ego, huh?" She laughed and turned until she showed Jenn her profile. "I can't believe you never recognized it."

Jenn blinked. "You mean…?"

"Yup. I had to choose a nose for the doctor so I chose yours. Remember when I blackmailed you to help me with that school project?"

"*That's* why you took all those pictures?"

"Would you have let me if I'd asked?"

"Probably not."

"Look, Jenn, I know we didn't always see eye to eye but those things I said to you…1 was a stupid little bitch and completely out of control. The point is, you look fantastic and Nick obviously loves you. If you're healthy, who cares what you weigh?"

Fresh tears appeared, accompanied by a smile. "That's what Nick says."

"Yeah? Well, if he ever says anything negative like Dad always did, you tell me and I'll kick his ass for you."

Jenn released a tearful laugh. "You'd do that?"

"Isn't that what big sisters are supposed to do?" She dropped another lock of curled hair and surveyed her work.

"You and Ethan…Things are good?"

She couldn't help the smile—or the sting of tears. "Yeah, they're good. I didn't know what this was like."

"What? Oh, my word. You're in love with him."

Megan opened her mouth to deny the claim but couldn't do it. "Is it always like this? Because I gotta tell you I'm really freaking out."

"Why are you asking me when—" Jenn broke off, her mouth opening in complete shock. "You mean you've never been in love? Ever? Your boyfriends? Not even when you married Sean?"

This was it. The moment she'd been waiting for. The perfect opportunity to unload and tell Jenn that Sean had raped her. But suddenly…it didn't matter. Right now, this moment, wasn't about the past and her stupid mistakes. It was about her and Jenn and sisterhood and the way they were talking right now. Now that she finally had it, she didn't want to ruin it.

"Love is terrifying," Jenn said softly, her lashes falling over her eyes. "Love makes you weak because those guys— They have such a power to hurt if they want to, and even though I know Nick will be happy about the baby, I'm so afraid."

"You're *pregnant?*"

A gorgeous smile transformed Jenn's features, but as quickly as it appeared, it fell. "We talked about kids but not about having one this soon. We just got married and Nick and Matt moved in and school started. I don't know how to tell Nick. And I know it's silly but I wanted to lose ten more pounds before we even started *trying.*"

"He'll be happy." The words were hard to say given the lump in her throat, but Megan managed to utter them. Happy for Jenn. She was so happy for Jenn, truly, but it hurt, too. "He'll be thrilled. After watching his family over Thanksgiving, it's obvious they all love kids." Feeling insanely awkward, Megan bent and hugged Jenn. "Stop worrying. Everything will be fine and you'll do great."

Jenn's lower lip trembled. "Thanks. And…I'm sorry, too. About the baby you lost."

She hadn't lost a baby. She'd lost two. Both miscarriages the result of Sean's abuse. But Jenn didn't know that. No one in her family even knew about the second pregnancy except her and Sean and the doctors and attorneys and judges involved in putting Sean away. Maybe one day she'd tell Jenn, but now wasn't the time. Now was a new memory. A happy memory between two sisters who hadn't been sisters for a long time.

Megan swallowed around that pesky lump as she moved behind Jenn and gathered her sister's hair into a loose handful. She twisted it then used a clip from Jenn's collection to fasten it on her head. Finished with that, she sprayed it then went to work repairing the mascara damage. "There. All finished for your wonderful night with Nick." She moved out of the way so Jenn could get a look in the mirror.

But Jenn didn't look at herself. She looked at Megan instead. "There's something you're not saying."

"It'll wait. Now say thank-you. I finished two minutes early despite major mascara removal." Megan started to turn only to have Jenn catch her hand and pull her back.

"Thank you."

"You're welcome. Come on. Let's get you dressed and the food ready so you can tell your guy *I'm* going to be an aunt."

SIMON'S EYES WIDENED when he saw Nemo swimming toward the boat. His mouth dropped open, and even though Megan had told Ethan that Simon had watched the movie before, Simon left his pillow and blanket behind and crawled onto Ethan's lap. He'd never get used to it, that fist-in-his-chest feeling that came every time Simon reached out to him. Thanks to Megan, it happened more and more often. A little hand in his, a nudge to look at something, a laugh when Simon helped Ethan cook breakfast.

"Nemo get lost."

Ethan patted the child's back. "But Nemo finds his daddy in the end, remember?"

Simon stared up at Ethan, his gaze searching. "Daddy...Ethan?"

The air whooshed from his lungs. Damn, but he felt as though he'd been sucker punched. He snuggled Simon close to his chest and hugged, hoping no one heard how husky his voice was. "Yeah. Daddy Ethan...or just Daddy. It's up to you, son. You can call me whatever yo—"

Ethan's pager went off the same time that his cell phone vibrated on his belt. He looked at the face, aware that Simon sighed in disappointment because he knew what it meant. Their perfect father-son moment had to end. "I'm sorry, bud, but we have to leave."

Like the trouper he was, Simon grabbed his pillow and blanket, then tucked his hand into Ethan's to go.

Chapter 20

"WHAT ABOUT MRS. DUNLEY? She requested you."

Two days later Ethan pressed the phone to his ear and stared at the surgery board. "The only available O.R. is on Tuesday at ten in the morning."

"You're in meetings from eight until four-thirty," his assistant, Shirley, reminded him.

He spied another opening. "What if we switched some things around?"

"Don't you touch that board. Last time somebody did that, the nurses went on strike. A balanced board is everything, you should know that."

He did know that, but how the hell was he supposed to perform surgery if he was in meetings all day? "Friday?"

"You're meeting the hospital board privately. They called to schedule this morning. I blocked off the whole day because Mr. Morrow said he wanted your full attention and it would take a while."

The whole day? His hand fisted over the phone. "Regarding?"

"If I had to guess, your job as chief. I wouldn't miss that one if I were you."

He couldn't miss any of them, that was the problem. "Schedule Mrs. Dunley with Dr. Woodruff. It's a simple gallbladder surgery. I'll be sure to stop by after the meeting and check on her."

"She's not going to be happy. You were the old gal's one request."

And he'd like to honor it. The woman had taught his father in grade school, then every one of his siblings, as well as himself, before retiring. When Mrs. Dunley spoke, you listened. "She can't wait another week to have this surgery. Her gallbladder isn't functioning as it is. One more bad attack and she could be in trouble." He heard Shirley scribbling notes. "That it?"

"For now. You doin' okay, honey? You're soundin' awfully tired."

"I'm fine," he said, taking a quote from his newest sister-in-law, Shelby, who said those two words repeatedly when she was anything but.

"It's not what you'd thought it would be, is it?"

He stared at the board, at the surgeries and the patients receiving care, noting that his name now rarely appeared in the sectioned-off blocks as the operating doctor. "Nope. I can't say that it is."

MEGAN STARED INTO THE DEPTHS of her take-out coffee cup while the library aid read a book involving a mouse and a cookie. The story was great—but it also sucked. It made her think of Ethan and how good he made chocolate-chip cookies and ice cream taste, and he'd worked so late every night this whole week that even when he got home, neither of them had the energy to do more than spoon. Any time they sat down to play a game with Simon, Ethan's pager went off, and that talk she still needed to have with Ethan? It hadn't happened.

It was just as well. Ever since Marilyn Tulane had invited Megan to join Darcy, Jenn and Rosetta for some marathon Christmas shopping and Megan had turned them down, Ethan had been giving her funny looks. He'd offered to give her money to pick some things up for Simon for Christmas and it would've been the perfect opportunity to spend time with Jenn, especially after their talk. But Megan hadn't gone. All because she couldn't explain the uneasy feeling she experienced whenever she was in town. Nearly every time she left the house. Thank goodness Ethan had taken her advice and cut back on Simon's schedule. Other than story hour, they spent most of their days at home.

It's nothing. You're freaking out over not being able to talk to Ethan about Sean and worrying about him spending so much time working. Concentrate on coming up with a cool Christmas present for Ethan, be productive and stop worrying over nothing.

Disgusted with herself, Megan tossed aside the latest issue of *Vanity Fair* and winced in apology when the librarian shot her a frown.

Megan got to her feet to stretch out the kinks in her back. Enough already. Give the kids their juice box and cookies and let's get the heck out of Dodge.

Moving to the window, she stared outside at the December landscape. Hard to believe she'd been here since October but Beauty had become home. She now knew Pete, the postmaster, Susie at swim class and twice now she'd taken Simon to visit Rosetta at her condo in The Village.

Movement across the street drew her attention and her

coffee threatened a return appearance. A dark bluejacket, sandy-blond hair.

Her insides froze, the breath leaking from her lungs like a pinpricked balloon. No. No, it wasn't. It *couldn't* be. Could it?

They were separated by glass and brick and two lanes of traffic, but something about the man was all too familiar. The tilt of his head, the way he walked. Memories slid over her like slime and a nasty curse appeared in her head, her heart pumping as if she'd run a marathon and hit the wall—or Sean's fist. "Simon, let's go."

Something about her voice had the other moms, grandmothers and babysitters in the room sending her worried glances. Megan forced a strained laugh and waved a hand toward the window. "It's snowing and I really don't like driving in the snow. It makes me nervous."

One of the grandmothers looked outside and back to her. "Oh, honey, it's just spittin' a little. Look at the sky. Give it five minutes and it'll peter out. The roads won't even be wet."

Hand to her forehead, she rubbed, grimacing. "No, I think we'd better go. I'm—I'm getting a migraine and need to lie down." Remembering an earlier trip to the bathroom, she turned to the librarian. "Do you have a back door? I hate to bother you but I parked in back. It would be so much easier if we could go out that way."

Seeing them all exchange a look that labeled her a drama queen, the librarian removed the glasses perched on her nose and let them dangle from the beaded lanyard around her neck. "Of course, sweetie. Simon, I hope to see you next time. Don't forget to reread the book and practice the words, okay?"

Megan hastily repeated the words in French and clutched Simon's coat in her hand. "Here we go, let's go," she said, prodding Simon along and practically mowing down the librarian as she slowly made her way to the rear of the building. Did the woman only have one speed?

"Thanks. Simon, hurry."

"Hon, are you all right?" Mrs. Bumgarner asked as she unlocked the back door.

"Peachy." Remembering her headache, which was now a true headache and not a fake one, she rubbed her temple again. "I just need some quiet. Thanks for letting us go out this way."

"Caring for a five-year-old can be difficult if you're not used to it. Should I call Ethan and tell him you're not feeling well?"

Ethan. She frowned at the familiarity. Oh, yeah, Mrs. B. had said she'd known the family for years, and even mentioned to her that Jenn had never talked about having a sister. Yeah, that hadn't hurt. "I'll be fine. Truly." She poked her head out and scanned the alley, thankful she *had* parked in the back. "We'll pop in a movie or read the book again once we get home."

"Well, be careful, dear."

"Thanks, I will."

Simon had remained blessedly silent during the exchange, and Megan flashed him a reassuring smile when she realized he stared at her, then glanced around them as though sensing danger.

He's a smart, perceptive kid. Of course he senses danger.

A loud beeping sound broke the mellow quiet and Megan started, belatedly realizing it was simply the warning signal of a truck reversing. She spotted the truck at the end of the alley where a guy was being lifted up to place wreaths on the lampposts. But beyond him on the street—Was that another flash of blue?

"Simon, *hurry.*" She herded the boy toward the Buick,

wishing for once in her life she liked sensible shoes instead of the heeled boots she wore. She unlocked the car and urged Simon inside where he scrambled into his booster seat. Megan grabbed the belt and fastened him in. She shut the door and opened the driver's door as quietly as possible, but out of the corner of her eye she saw the man in blue turn toward them.

"Megan?"

Oh, Lord. Oh, Please. Megan kept her head averted and scrambled inside. With a twist of the key and Nick's blessed intervention to repair her car, the old Buick started with a roar.

MEGAN COULDN'T STOP PACING, peeking out the window and blessing the inventor of blinds. She'd parked her car inside the garage and put the door down. She'd checked to make sure it was down. Twice. Blinds shut, doors locked. Alarm system on.

Ethan will be home soon. Stop freaking out.

But how could she tell him now? Saying she was married and that it had been bad was one thing, but to have the ex-husband show up on Ethan's doorstep? What guy wanted to deal with that when Ethan was already dealing with so much?

She'd brought Simon home from the library and fed him, bathed him, then put him to bed after a round of television that frayed the last of her nerves because the cartoon noises exploded out of the television like someone bursting into the house.

Sean was here, in Beauty. And it was all her fault. She'd led a violent man to the people she cared about and loved more than anything in the world.

And Simon. Poor Simon. Instead of curling up in bed and closing his eyes, he'd given her a steady stare and asked if she'd seen the mean man. Simon had told her not to be scared because he would *protect* her. How sweet was that? But she knew Sean, and nothing, especially not a little boy, could protect her. In fact, if Sean truly wanted to hurt her, threatening Ethan and Simon or Jenn was the ultimate way to do it.

The low rumble of a vehicle reached her ears and she peeked out once more. Ethan's SUV pulled into the driveway and as much as she wanted Ethan home, now… Now she wished she had more time, because once he walked in that door and he realized what she'd done, there was no going back.

She moved through the darkened house to the interior entry door to turn off the alarm system and unlock the door, hearing the metal garage door rumble up then down. Her heart thumped so hard in her chest it hurt to breathe, but she couldn't let herself back down. She'd done this, now she had to take responsibility for it.

A deeply ridged frown marred Ethan's handsome features as he crossed the threshold and her fingers itched to reach out and smooth it away. Ethan was visibly tired, exhausted from the long hours and responsibilities he held. He needed someone to support him and all he tried to accomplish, not bring him down by dumping more problems on him. She hated herself right now. Thanks to her, they were all in danger.

"Hey." Ethan dropped a quick kiss on her lips but kept going.

Megan blinked. "Ethan?"

He paused, but now that he was there, words left her. How did she tell the man she loved that she'd allowed another man to *beat* her, for years? It didn't matter that

Sean was larger and stronger, that she wasn't responsible for Sean's actions during their marriage. All that mattered was that it had happened, and she'd stayed with him and endured the abuse for much, much too long because she was too stubborn and embarrassed to seek help. She'd actually convinced herself for a while that Sean would get better, that maybe, just maybe, she'd gotten what she deserved, whatever Sean dished out. She'd stayed because of her pride. With her, it always came back to pride. And now here she was being taken down again.

"I need to talk to you." She turned and walked into the utility room so that they weren't standing in the hall where they might possibly wake Simon. What to do, what to say?

"Sweetheart, I've had a hell of a day and I just want to crash. Can't it wait?"

"No."

"Did Simon do something wrong?"

Tears burned her eyes and she blinked them away. She'd lost two babies thanks to Sean. Now a third. "No. No, he was perfect," she said thickly. Absolutely perfect. A loving child, giving and sweet. *Hers*. In all the ways that mattered most, Simon was hers.

"Then whatever it is can wait until morning. It's been a lousy day." Ethan turned to exit the utility room.

"No! Ethan, stop. It *can't* wait. I'm leaving."

Chapter 21

ETHAN STOPPED and pivoted back to her, surprise and wariness stamped on his features, like he braced himself for some sick punch line. Jenn was right. She wasn't good for Simon, wasn't good for Ethan. And sometimes, the best thing you could do for the people you loved was just to let them be.

Without a word, Megan closed the distance between them in rapid, panic-driven steps. She plastered herself against him, cradled his face in her palms and kissed him. One last time. Eyes open, she could see the concern and frustration in his expression, but she had to shut him up and have one last taste or she'd never have the courage to say what had to be said. Because when he knew the truth he'd never look at her the same, never think of her the same. Even though people said it doesn't matter what others think, it did matter. It mattered a lot.

She kissed him with all the need and want inside her, with all the happiness and exasperation and hope he had instilled in her, however short-lived.

Ethan's arms went around her, lifted her, his body

hardening against her hips. She wasn't a wallflower-virgin. But this was nothing like anything she'd experienced, and she knew it—knew *love*—would never come around again. Not like this. This was life, breath. Pain. It was dancing in the rain and laughing in bed and making out like teenagers.

But what kind of person would she be if she expected a father to overlook the fact that she'd endangered his son? By coming here and selfishly using them to hide out, she'd put a child and her pregnant sister in danger and that wasn't the person she wanted to be.

It took all the strength within her, but Megan managed to stomp down the scream inside her trying to break free and ended the kiss, her heart hurting in a way it never had before.

"Megan? Sweetheart, what's wrong? What happened? Something with you and Jenn?"

She squeezed out a smile, determined to keep the people she loved safe. She wasn't a heroine too stupid to live in some poorly penned adventure novel. She was strong, she was smart and she would fight Sean with everything in her. But first she'd protect her family.

"Megan, come on, you're scaring me. What's wrong?"

"When I came here, all I thought about was myself. I didn't care that Jenn didn't want me here. I didn't care that I was sick or that my presence would inconvenience anyone, or that it might—It might hurt her marriage." She untangled herself from his embrace and retreated, holding up her hands when he stepped forward, arms outstretched. "And I didn't…I didn't come here just to apologize to Jenn, either."

The confession came out in a say-it-now-or-choke-on-it rush. She couldn't look at him, couldn't stand to see the disappointment and disgust in Ethan's eyes. Honesty was important to him. Honesty, loyalty. Family and faith. He was a good man, and she didn't want him knowing what Sean had done to her. It was embarrassing and sad; it made her feel weak and stupid, just as her father had always said she was.

"Then why did you come?"

"I came because…" *Tell the truth.* "I came to use Jenn. I —I came here because I needed help and I knew Jenn wouldn't turn me away."

His eyebrows pulled low. "But she did."

And Megan had wound up relying on and using Ethan's kindness and generosity instead.

His expression changed. Frustration gave way to out-and-out wariness, his body tensing, hands fisted at his sides.

She saw the fists but she wasn't afraid. He would use his fists on himself before he would ever lift them to her in punishment, no matter how angry he was over being deceived. But the wariness, the dawning understanding of who she truly was—who she'd been—and the lies she'd told by omission, that was hard to witness.

"You've been using me. That's what you're saying?"

"I had nowhere to go," she whispered, mortified. "I ran out of money and got sick. I was sleeping in my car." Oh, the expression on his face. It hurt to see him look at her with such pity. "I couldn't go to my parents and Jenn's house was the closest, anyway, and I thought—Ethan, I never would have risked it had I known that he'd follow me here."

His expression darkened even more. "Risked what? What are you talking about? Who followed you?"

"Sean."

"Your ex-husband?"

She nodded, her hands gripping her arms so hard that she knew she'd have bruises tomorrow. "He's *here*."

Ethan stared at her in silence, anger stamped on his features. He moved close, until he nudged her to look him in the eyes.

"I know you were sleeping in your car, and I know you had nowhere else to go. It didn't take a scientist to figure that out. Now tell me what's going on. All of it."

He knew? And he'd taken her in, trusted her anyway? *It's the type of man he is. A good man.* Which made it harder to say, "He's out of prison."

"Prison?"

"Assault, and more charges. When he got drunk, he got violent." She lowered her lashes, staring at Ethan's chin. "He got drunk a lot, and the last time it happened…Sean tried to kill me."

"Dear God."

"He vowed that when he got out, he'd find me. That I'd pay for pressing charges and putting him there." Oh, this was so hard, harder than she'd ever imagined. "He said—He said he would find me. After I filed for divorce I moved, and I kept moving. I changed addresses, changed cities. Nine times in two years because I was afraid…When I got sick I thought of Jenn." She lowered her head. "I hoped Jenn would forgive me and I knew Jenn's was the last place Sean would look."

"But Sean figured it out and he's followed you here?"

Megan gripped Ethan's wrist, but whether it was to pull his hand away or hold it against her cheek she wasn't sure. Scenes flashed through her head. The past. Instances like this where Sean had grabbed her jaw or neck and squeezed, choked her, hurt her. While Ethan just stood there looking as though she'd betrayed him. And hadn't she? "I'm sorry. I'm *so* sorry."

Ethan dropped his hand and stared at her, the furrow between his eyebrows deepening. "You've known all this time, been here all this time, and you didn't *once* think you should have told us—*me*—that you could be in danger?"

"I thought I'd be able to leave before Sean ever thought to come here." It was a lousy excuse and she knew it. It didn't matter that she hadn't planned to stay, she had stayed, thinking of Beauty as her safe place when there wasn't one. She shook her head, wanting to plead with Ethan to forgive her but understanding that he couldn't. "But he's here. Ethan, I saw him."

"Where? When?"

"Today. He was outside the library. I made an excuse and took Simon out the back, but—he saw me. He called my name. Sean was far enough away that I ignored him and took off."

"We have to call the police."

Ethan turned on his heel and left the utility room. Megan's trembling legs carried her to the door, and she watched as he hurried down the hall. She waited, torn, until she heard his voice talking to a 911 operator, trying to explain the situation.

But she knew what she had to do. With Ethan distracted, she slipped out the door to the garage. Everything was loaded and ready to go. Now that Ethan knew the truth, he could protect Simon. He'd tell Nick and Nick would protect Jenn. They'd be safe. They'd all be safe, because she wouldn't be there.

Megan pressed her fingers to her mouth and held them there. To hold in the taste of Ethan's kiss, to hold back the cry of his name and the words that didn't matter now. She'd saved every dime Ethan had paid her. She'd travel north. Maybe go to Chicago like she'd planned or south to Palm Beach. She could wait tables at L'Escalier. If she needed help along the way she'd contact the police there, but not in Beauty. Not where it would embarrass or hurt the people she loved.

The important thing was that since she didn't know where she was going, how could Sean follow?

"THIS CAN'T BE HAPPENING." Megan stared down at the flat driver's-side front tire and shivered. A drizzling rain fell from the sky and seeped into the material of her coat, and all she could think about was the irony of how the last two times she'd tried to run from something, her car had broken down. *Maybe because it's time you stop running? Go back and see what happens. You know Ethan will help you.*

She kicked the stupid flat tire. "*Ow. Sh—Crap,*" she corrected automatically, in the habit of watching her language because she usually had Simon in tow.

No cars had passed for a while. One older woman had driven by when it had first happened but she hadn't stopped. Not that Megan could blame her. Who would stop in this day and age? With no streetlights, the country roads were freaking dark. She wouldn't have stopped, either.

Megan muttered to herself as she stomped back to the trunk. The tire iron and jack were dirty and bulky, but she set to work on changing the tire herself, not that she had a clue what she was doing.

After twenty minutes the only thing she'd managed to accomplish was to give herself blisters from trying to pry the stupid lug nuts or bolts or whatever they were called off the wheels and to have broken three nails.

Lights flickered through the trees and she turned, blinking the rain out of her eyes as she watched a car round the bend. The headlights blinded her but whoever was behind the wheel signaled and pulled onto the shoulder behind the Buick. Megan watched, leery but hopeful, as the driver's door opened. Then her smile fell and her past returned. "Oh, Lord, no," she whispered. "God, please. Not again. I can't do this again."

Sean walked to the hood of his car and with every step the fear built. Her nose ran, mascara burned her eyes —but her grip on the tire iron turned into a white-knuckled fist. If she went down, she'd go down with a fight.

Sean held up his hands. "It's okay, Meggie."

"Get b-back in your car and k-keep going."

He looked at the metal rod, his expression clearly wondering if she had the nerve to use it.

"Let me change the tire for you."

"Go to the devil."

He flashed the smile that had won him the hearts of girls and mothers alike. "Nicer than telling me to go to hell." He yanked at the zipper of his coat and pulled the hood over his head. "Get in the car."

"Go. *Away*."

"I'm freezing out here and so are you. You want to stand here and yell at me or get your tire changed? You don't have a lot of choices."

"I'll do it myself."

"Why? Get in the car, lock the doors and toss the tire iron out the window once you're safe so I can change the tire."

He said it so reasonably. "How stupid would I be to give this to you?"

Did his face soften? "I won't hurt you, Meggie."

"Since when?"

Sean actually seemed to look ashamed. "You have no

reason to believe me, I know that. But I'm telling the truth. Get in the car before you catch pneumonia."

She wasn't sure what to do. They both knew he could get the tire iron from her if he decided to try. If she got a shot in, it would be her one and only before he overtook her. Megan released a hefty gush of air from her lungs. "Back up, all the way to the end of your car."

Surprisingly he did as ordered without complaint.

Megan opened her car door, climbed in and immediately locked the door. He didn't move, not until he saw her roll down the window far enough to toss the tool out of the vehicle.

Rain beat down on Sean as he retrieved the iron and dropped down to look at the tire. She knew what he saw. The bolts were rusted in place. By the time he had the bolts loosened, the tire changed and everything back in her trunk, he was soaked through and his knees were covered in mud.

He shut the trunk lid, his pace slow and his hands visible as he walked to the driver's window. Like he tried not to scare her. What a joke.

"Megan? It's done. Don't take off. Meggie, please," he begged when she reached for the keys. "Hear me out."

The bright beams of his car filled her vehicle and lit his face, erasing shadows, giving her the full brunt of his expression. She watched him, reliving every moment of their time together. The things he'd said to her, the things he'd done. The bruises she'd hidden and even the ones she hadn't been able to disguise.

"Roll down the window. Please."

She shook her head firmly. Maybe he'd changed her tire and maybe he'd put the tire iron back in her trunk, but she wasn't an idiot.

Sean lowered his hands to the base of her window and Megan stiffened. His chapped hands were bleeding.

"Don't be afraid."

It was hard to hear over the rain pounding the roof of the car but she heard those three words and strangely enough, a sense of peace filled her.

"Meggie? Don't be afraid," he repeated. "I know you won't believe this, but I'm not here to frighten you or threaten you or hurt you."

Megan's hands tightened on the wheel, on the gearshift. She had to part her lips to take in more air.

"Just listen, okay? Please, darlin', I need you to hear me." Sean lowered his head, chin to chest, the rain washing over his head, his neck, the blood on his hands. "I'm sorry. I am so sorry. I'm not here to ask you back, Meggie. And I didn't find you because I want to hurt you. I did it because I had to…I had to apologize."

She looked at him, totally disbelieving.

"You were right. I am an alcoholic. I've been an alcoholic since I was fifteen."

She didn't respond, unable to believe what she was hearing.

"I've joined A.A. I'm sober, and I plan to stay this way. I scared you, I *hurt* you and I know it. I did you wrong and there aren't any excuses that will take back what I did. But I am more sorry than you'll ever know."

Why? Why now?

"Something happened. Something I can't explain. But I'm not the same person I was. I'm not here to hurt you, Meggie. I just—You're number one on my list. You're the person I hurt the most. You're the one…" His head lowered even more and he trembled, his breath white in the night air. "You're the one I *owe* the most. I wanted you to know that it's over. I had to see you in person and apologize, and tell you that I won't bother you again."

Sean lifted one of his bloody hands and flattened it gently against the window. He didn't push, didn't shove, didn't hit. Why couldn't he have shown her this gentleness during their marriage?

"Goodbye, Meggie."

Just like that he pulled his hand from the glass and walked away.

Megan sat there a moment until the rage boiling inside her got the better of her. She opened her door and got out, just enough that she could see him, call his name. "Why?" Rain or tears streamed down her face, she wasn't sure which. Wasn't sure what to believe. "Why couldn't you write me a letter? Why not leave a message on the stupid answering machine? Why now?"

Chapter 22

"YOU MOVED A LOT," Sean called back. He dipped his head once again. "And I had to make sure you're okay."

Okay? *Okay?* A strangled laugh bubbled out of her chest, choked and caustic and full of fury. She'd run off in the middle of a storm, at night, because she was terrified and he thought that was okay?

"Go home, Megan. Go back to Jenn and that guy you've been working for."

She stiffened, her whole body going ramrod-straight. "Don't you go near them!"

"I'm leaving town soon as I get a tank full of gas." He lifted his chin toward the car. "Where were you going?"

She didn't answer, couldn't. Because she wasn't sure now. She felt the way she had once way back when in gymnastics. She'd made a run for the vault and screwed up, and the next thing she knew she was on the floor unable to breathe. It was a horrible feeling, mouth open, trying to suck in air but it wouldn't come. She felt like that now. Breathless, scared. Unsure.

"Tell him what I did to you," Sean ordered, his voice carrying over the rain and bouncing eerily off the trees and asphalt surrounding them. "Tell him what I did and where your mind is. He'll understand. If he doesn't, he isn't worth your time."

Was this real? It didn't feel real. The whole scene, Sean, it was like something from a dream. But she knew she wasn't dreaming because it hurt too much. After all those years, was this what sober looked like? Tired, calm, caring. Sad and yet—free?

"Goodbye, Meggie." His lips curled at the corners in a handsome smile. "I wish you a good life."

"CAN I HELP—SEAN?"

At the sound of Jenn's startled exclamation, Ethan hurried down the hallway toward Nick and Jenn's front door. If Sean had hurt Megan so help him he'd—

Nick caught him before Ethan could get there and yank the door out of Jenn's hand.

"Let's figure out why he's here," Nick said softly.

"Hey, Jenn. You look nice."

Nick stiffened and Ethan smirked. If Sean flirted with Jenn, Nick would take the guy's head off—and since Nick had the brutal power to do it, Ethan wouldn't mind being second in line. Much.

"I'm sure you're wondering why I'm here."

"I assume it has something to do with Megan. She's not here."

"I know. She had a flat outside town. I changed it for her."

Then where was she now?

"Look, I was wondering if I could talk to you? Explain some things. Will you hear me out?"

Ethan wanted to go to the door and give Sean a taste of his own medicine, but Nick and now Luke both held him by his arms. Jenn glanced at them and Nick whispered for her to find out where Megan was.

"Jenn…I drank over half my life," Sean said softly. "My old man had a bar in the house for his buddies, but we all know it worked for teenagers, too, remember?"

Jenn nodded slowly.

"I was the big man in school with that bar. Toss in fast cars and easy money, and by the time I was a freshman in college I could outdrink the five-year frat boys. I partied hard."

"You and Megan both. But why are you telling me this?"

From behind the sheer-curtained window, Ethan saw Sean lower his head. "Because…Here's the thing…I'm not proud of how I behaved now. I wound up flunking and instead of wising up and changing my ways, I sweet-talked you into doing the work for me. All that stuff Megan said about me dating you? I hate to say it but it was true."

"I see."

Sean shoved his hands into his pockets and even though he stood under the stoop, Ethan noticed he was soaking wet.

"I'm sorry. I mean it, too. I'm in A.A. now, which is why I'm here. To set things right with Meggie, and with you and Meggie because of what I did to the two of you. You know, after she set me up."

"She slept with you."

Ethan narrowed his gaze, watching as Sean stared at his feet, head down, shoulders bowed. "No, she didn't," he said huskily.

"Sean, she got pregnant, of course she did."

Sean's nostrils flared and he shuffled on his feet, seemingly unable to raise his head. "Like I said, I'm not proud of how I behaved or what I did to her."

"What you *did* to her?" Jenn whispered.

"Jenn, I made her. Forced her." A shudder rocked the man's shoulders. "I'm sorry."

It took Nick and Luke to keep Ethan from barreling out the door. Sean had *raped* her?

"You know what happened after she got pregnant," Sean continued when Jenn remained silent.

Ethan wondered if Sean had a death wish, if he knew Ethan and his brothers were on the other side of the door waiting on him to finish his confession so they could lay him out.

"She didn't know what to do and you know how your parents and mine reacted." Sean cleared his throat, the sound rough, and wiped his hand under his nose.

Were his knuckles bloody?

"I don't remember much about our wedding day. Only that I woke up on my honeymoon in Mexico."

"Sean."

"I know." The words were guttural, broken, but he raised his gaze to Jenn, eyes red-rimmed and flooded with tears.

Ethan hardened his heart at the sight. The doctor in him understood the ramifications of addiction, but the man in him was furious at what Megan had endured at Sean's hands.

"There is nothing you can say to me that I haven't already said to myself. Nothing you can think that I haven't —I'm sorry."

"What happened to the baby? What really happened?"

Jenn demanded hotly. "Megan told me you hurt her, that you hit her. Is that why she miscarried?"

Ethan shut his eyes, able to picture the scene all too well. The hell Megan had gone through, survived. She'd told Jenn. Why hadn't she told him?

"No. Not that first time. They said it was stress. But the second time…That was my fault. That's why I wound up going to prison. She said she was leaving and I—I tried to hurt her."

Nick shoved Ethan into Luke's hold in time to keep Jenn from flying toward Sean. Garret quickly took Nick's place, and Ethan winced at the broken cry Jenn released.

Ethan jerked his arms loose from his brothers' and moved to the crowded doorway, Garret and Luke at his heels.

"Nick, let me go! You heard what he did!"

Sean's gaze met his the moment Ethan came into view, and Ethan knew by the man's expression that Sean recognized him. Sean swallowed but made no move to defend himself.

"If I could do things over, I would."

"But you *can't*. How could you?" Jenn's voice was raw with tears, pain.

Ethan never took his eyes off Megan's ex-husband. "Where's Megan?"

"I changed her tire and left like I told her I would. She was still sitting by the side of the road outside town when I came here." The man stared down at the tattoo inscribed on the inside of his wrist. Above the number was a small cross and two teardrops. "I paid for what I did."

"Nothing could ever pay for that," Jenn said with a choked sob. "A couple years in prison is *nothing* for doing what you did. For murder! You should've been dealt the same hand you gave to Megan and her babies."

Nick soothed his wife but apparently knew better than to try to get Jenn back inside the house.

Sean nodded in what appeared to be total agreement. "I know. Jenn, I know that. It sounds crazy but…1 agree. Look, a guy in prison lost his wife and baby to a drunk driver who just mowed them over on the guy's front lawn. The drunk got off with time served, so Junior took things into his own hands and went to prison. When Junior heard what I'd—why I was there, he beat the hell out of me every chance he could. Got so bad the warden put us in side-by-side cells, trying to make us get along."

Sean lifted his gaze to Jenn and, like it or not, Ethan saw the pain, the sincerity, of his words.

But he still wanted to beat Sean the same way Junior had.

"Did you?" Garret asked.

"Eventually. The hardest part wasn't the beatings. I know it sounds crazy, but the hardest part was listening to Junior pray." He ran a hand over his forehead. "Night after night Junior would sit on his bunk and read his Bible out loud. Then he'd start talking—praying—for me. One day when I was on the ground at Junior's feet, something finally clicked." Sean inhaled. "That's why I'm here. Look, all I wanted was to set the record straight and smooth things over with you and Meggie. It wasn't her fault. None of it. I did the things she said. I did more than that," he said, shamefaced. "Kept her from calling, told her she was dead to all of you. I thought you needed to hear that from me, since you probably wouldn't believe that coming from her."

JENN'S HOUSE was something out of a magazine.

Little candle lights in each window of the saltbox, the wreath lit on the door. A beautiful tree framed perfectly in the picture window.

Megan stared at the tree, unsure of what to do or where to go now. Sean had pulled away and kept driving down the road after his little speech, and she'd climbed back into her car and sat there a long time, shocked, stunned, digesting his words and finally realizing that this was how Jenn must have felt when she'd suddenly appeared in Beauty. She'd wanted Jenn to give her a second chance, wanted Jenn's forgiveness, and there Sean was, wanting the same thing.

"Oh, the irony," Megan whispered, staring up at the sky. "You're good."

She'd tried to drive by Beauty and keep going but couldn't. Now here she sat, staring at Jenn's home, still trying to catch her breath. She felt like a fish. All these years she'd been caught on a hook and she'd thrashed and flailed, reacting to her father, to her mother, Jenn, Sean and the miscarriages and all that had happened.

But she was tired of thrashing, tired of hanging from that stupid hook and she wanted a home. A family. A new start. A life where she was Megan, not Megs or Meggie.

She'd come to Beauty under false pretenses. To get well, hide, and if she were honest, to rub Jenn's nose in what Megan had endured on her sister's behalf as though Jenn owed her for something she didn't even know had occurred. In that sense, Megan knew her thoughts weren't rational but those of the child she'd been. Once here, she'd realized it didn't matter, not anymore. Jenn would probably never understand the complexity of her decision or the anger Megan had held inside, but she didn't need to know. It had been Megan's decision, her choice. Her life to live.

She ached with wanting to go knock on that door and

talk to Jenn, laugh with her, be the sisters they were supposed—but never had been allowed—to be. How could she face Jenn now? And Ethan—Maybe Sean wasn't the monster he'd been, maybe he wasn't stalking her with the violence of the past, but how could Ethan possibly—

The door to Jenn and Nick's house opened and people spilled out. Not just Ethan but also Luke, Garret and Alan as well as Tobias Richardson and several of the cousins she remembered from Thanksgiving dinner. But why were they all there? Together?

Garret and Tobias had climbed into Garret's SUV while her attention had been on the others. Garret swung the vehicle out of the drive, the bright headlights flashing over her car where she'd parked along the street in a shadowy area. The lights blinded her but nothing could've kept her from hearing Ethan's hoarse shout.

Unsure of what to do, she fumbled for the keys, even though spots danced in front of her eyes due to the bright lights. But it was too late.

In a matter of seconds everything changed. She heard the roar of an engine as Garret gunned the motor and headed right toward her, squealing to a stop and blocking her exit. Ethan ran toward her, skidding to a halt when he reached the car.

"Megan? Open the door. Megan, open the door!"

Chapter 23

TREMBLING UNCONTROLLABLY, Megan pulled the lock up. Two seconds later Ethan was in the car with her, releasing her seat belt and pulling her out of the vehicle into his arms.

"Oh, thank God."

"What's wrong? Is Simon okay? Did something happen? Where's Jenn?"

Ethan had buried his nose in her hair and at her words he squeezed her so tight the air squeaked from her lungs.

"He's fine. She's fine."

She couldn't tell which of them was trembling more, her or Ethan, but when she opened her eyes the rest of the Tulanes had gathered around them in the middle of the rain-soaked street.

Ethan drew back and shifted his hands to her face, his eyes glittering beneath the streetlight. "Are you all right? We were just leaving to search for you."

"But...why?" she whispered. "I told you what I'd done, that Sean had followed me."

He pulled her back into his arms and kissed her

temple, her hair. "And you scared ten years off my life by taking off like that. When we talked to Sean—"

"You *talked* to Sean?" She pushed at his confining arms. "When?"

Ethan released her enough that she could look up at him, but he kept her tight to his side, like he had to have contact.

Jenn moved closer toward Megan and Ethan. "Megan, why didn't you tell us you were running from him?"

The knot in Megan's stomach returned with force. "Jenn, I swear I didn't think he'd come here."

"But why didn't you tell us so we could help you?"

Megan looked at the faces surrounding her and saw fierce loyalty etched on every one of them. Her heart broke. She'd wanted a family for so long, wanted to belong, and here she was an honorary member as Simon's nanny. But she'd abused their trust in the worst way. "I was scared," she managed to whisper. "I knew you didn't want me here and if I told you that…I had to see you, to say I was sorry."

"In case Sean caught up with you?"

"Yes."

"In case he *hurt* you?" Jenn pressed, horrified.

Big tears filled her eyes that no dam could hold back. With a gasp Jenn closed the distance between them in two steps and Ethan released her as Jenn's arms surrounded her.

"The things he did to you. Oh, Megan."

Eyes closed, she relished the feel of Jenn hugging her. "It was what it was." She smoothed her hand over Jenn's hair, just as she used to do before the madness of sibling rivalry kicked in. "I'm sorry I came. Jenn, I never would've endangered you or the baby. I would die before I'd let that happen, please believe that."

"*Ahem*. I, uh, think we need to go inside," Alan said from the sidelines, emotion clogging his voice.

"We'll be in in a minute. Nick, pry your wife off and calm her down. Jenn, she's fine, she's here, and she's not going anywhere. Are you, sweetheart?"

Nick plucked Jenn's arms from around her and gave Jenn a comforting squeeze. "Come on, babe. The sooner they talk, the sooner you can hug Megan again."

Ethan turned to face her fully, but Megan was very aware that none of his family moved. They all watched. Listened.

"Promise me you won't *ever* pull a stunt like that again. If you have a problem, *we* have a problem. You scared the hell out of me when I realized you'd left."

"I'm sorry." She sounded like a broken record. "I was…trying to do the responsible thing. I knew if I left, Sean would follow me and you'd all be safe."

"Megan…did I scare you tonight, with my response? Is that why you ran instead of trusting me to help you?"

She closed her eyes and leaned against him, exhausted physically and emotionally. "No. No," she repeated, raising her head so that she could look him in the eyes, careful to keep her voice low. She had a lot of explaining to do to Ethan and Jenn, but she didn't want to do it on the street. And it would take time. Time she now had with them? "You've had plenty of opportunity to hurt me if you wanted. I know you'd never lift a hand to me."

"We'd set him straight if he ever made you think he would," Garret informed her.

"In the old days the neighboring men would get together and set a bundle of sticks on the porch."

The group as a whole turned to stare at Tobias Richardson in confusion.

Realizing he'd gained everyone's attention, Garret's

best friend shrugged. "Just saying. It was a signal to the man of the house that he was being watched and if his wife and kids were abused again, they'd use the sticks on him."

Ethan sighed at being interrupted and Megan found herself wishing for privacy more than ever.

"Megan, I know you would never have put Simon at risk."

"But I did. I didn't mean to but I did."

"No, you didn't. I was upset by the news but only because you hadn't told me you needed help, not because I thought you'd risked Simon. You *threw up* at the idea of Simon thinking he had to eat dirt cookies, and you left town the moment you realized your ex-husband was here. Those aren't the traits of someone who'd put her interests above someone she loves, that was you protecting him."

"You were angry. You can't deny that."

"Of course I was angry. I was angry because Mrs. Dunley didn't make it through her surgery today."

He'd told her about his former teacher, how sweet she was. How upset he was that he couldn't perform her operation. "Oh, Ethan. I'm so sorry." No wonder he'd been in such a mood.

"I know these things happen, but I was angry as hell that it had to happen to her. I've been so busy doing administrative crap and sitting through meetings that I scheduled her surgery with another doctor when she requested me."

"I know." She smoothed her hands over his chest. "But, Ethan, you can't blame yourself for that. She might have died no matter who performed the surgery."

"I know. But today it hit home that I've been chasing a dream I don't really want. That's why I told the hospital board to take me out of the running for chief. When I think of the time I've wasted with you and Simon, I get angry all over again."

"Oh, Ethan, are you sure? You're giving up the promotion?" Jenn asked.

"You're upset." Megan fingered his coat. "With me and with Mrs. Dunley's death, maybe now isn't the time to make decisions."

He dropped a kiss to her lips, lingering over the contact. "It's the perfect time. I thought I wanted it, but I found out today what I really want. I love what I do as a doctor and surgeon, not sitting at a desk or in a meeting. I want to operate, but I want a life, too. I want to raise my son, be a father and share all that with the woman I love."

The air left her lungs in a rush. "Love?"

He framed her face with his hands. "Love," he repeated softly. "Will you stay, Megan? We'll take things slow, get to know each other better and do things right, but please, don't go."

"I want you to stay, too." Jenn smiled. "My baby will need you to teach her all that girlie stuff I don't know."

"And Simon needs a mother," Luke said as he rejoined the group, carrying Simon in his arms. Luke was followed closely by Marilyn, a relieved smile of welcome on her gently lined face.

Simon was dressed in his pajamas but the moment he saw them, he shoved at Luke's shoulders to be put down. His slippers made a scratching sound on the asphalt as Simon ran toward them. Ethan scooped the boy up into his arms only to give Simon to Megan before wrapping them both in his embrace.

"What do you say?" Ethan asked softly. "We need you, sweetheart. We love you. Are you ready to be part of our family?"

Megan laughed softly. Her chest hurt it was so full, her

heart ready to explode with love. She raised her mouth to Simon's ear and whispered to the boy, drawing a giggle from him.

"Well, Simon?" Ethan smiled at them both. "What did Mommy Megan say?"

With his little arms looped around her neck, Simon grinned from ear to ear. "Mommy say yes!"

Epilogue

Eight months later

SHE SHOULD HAVE REALIZED her perfect big sister would one day grow up to be the perfect doctor's wife, with the perfect house in the country, the perfect family and the perfect business growing by leaps and bounds. It was all so…

"Perfect," Jenn said with a smile.

She pulled up in front of Simon Says Day Care & Preschool. She never would have believed it possible for Megan to have chosen this career for herself. But Jenn had to admit her sister had the patience of a saint when dealing with the children. She was fun and creative, and she'd already made a name for herself in town, so much so everyone wanted their children enrolled in Simon's namesake.

"There you are," Megan said when Jenn entered the brightly painted door. "I was beginning to think you were taking her with you."

"I wish I could." Jenn sighed and kissed Rosie, not wanting to leave her daughter for her first day back at school but knowing without a doubt her baby girl was in good hands. Megan wasn't the teenager of years ago and after Megan and Ethan had married at Easter, they'd gotten a little surprise of their own. Simon's little sister would be born around Christmas and the girl cousins wouldn't be far apart in age.

And since she was nearly back to her prebaby weight and still going down thanks to good old-fashioned nursing, she couldn't wait to be the skinny sister and rub it in when Megan waddled like a duck.

Megan pried Rosie from her grasp and settled the baby against her chest like a pro.

Jenn smoothed her fingers over Rosie's cheek and kissed her repeatedly.

"Jenn, enough already. You're going to smother her."

"You'll call me if—"

"Yes."

"And you have all the numbers if—"

"Yes."

"You—"

"Yes, yes, *yes!* Rosie will be fine and if we have any questions or problems, I'll call. Immediately."

Jenn noted the way Megan made goofy faces at an oblivious Rosie. Rosie would be all right. Just as she and Megan would be all right. They still argued over everything but things were different now, better than they ever had been, and she knew it was because they'd learned to talk to each other. They'd learned to coexist, protected each other's back to anyone who dared to say a negative thing and could put themselves in each other's shoes—not that she'd ever be able to wear those ridiculous spikes Megan preferred.

"You know, Nick said if you refused to leave he'd come carry you out."

"Oh, hush. You wouldn't call him."

"Would, too." Megan shot her a superior, older-sibling look. "Jenn, you're late for work. Get out."

Jenn huffed but acknowledged the time crunch. "Bye, lovebug." She leaned close and kissed Rosie again. "You be good and remember what Mommy told you. If Aunt Megan is mean?" she said sweetly, sliding Megan a playful glare. "You have my permission to pee on her."

I HOPE YOU ENJOYED THE DOCTOR'S NANNY. KEEP READING BELOW FOR AN EXCERPT OF *A HERO IN HIDING*, THE NEXT BOOK IN THE TENNESSEE TULANES SERIES BY IVY JAMES.

IT'S SO SMALL. DOESN'T HE realize size matters? What if he can't get it up, what am I going to do then?

Alexandra Tulane swallowed nervously and forced a confident smile to her lips while she tried to figure out the best way of getting the job done. Climb aboard, close her eyes and pray for the quickest ride ever? Or take things nice and slow?

Slow won't get it up. And isn't the saying, It's not the size but what the guy can do with it?

Her inner voice snickered. Oh, if that's the case, you'd better hope he's really good.

Alex pressed her fingers to her lips to hold back a near-hysterical laugh. She'd gone off the deep end. No doubt about it, the stress had finally gotten to her. What else could explain her standing here having a complete conversation with herself?

She tore her attention from the dark-haired pilot striding away from the pathetically small plane outside the terminal window and looked around the airport, trying to stomp down the fear churning inside her. She didn't *do* small planes and the one tied to the pier and *floating* beneath the cloudy late-October sky was just short of matchbox size.

No way would everyone in the waiting area fit on there. What were they thinking? Even she knew planes couldn't fly too heavy or they would—she gulped—*crash*.

In all of her travels she'd been very blessed to avoid puddle jumpers holding fewer than fifty people. That is, until now. From what she could see the Deadwood Mountain Lodge logoed plane only had four, maybe six, seats. It gave new meaning to the word *tiny*.

Her destination was located along Chakachama Lake and touted as being Alaska's guy paradise, "froufrouless, rustic and lacking fluff." As a writer/reviewer for Traveling Single, she'd reviewed everything from B and B's and inns to five-star hotels and resorts, and had a fabulous time doing it.

But to get to the lodge, was she really going to have to get on *that?*

David tried to warn you but you refused to listen.

Yeah, well, what could her boss *really* know about it? David was a great businessman and had seen the magazine through hard economic times by adding an online subscription e-zine, but he was an armchair traveler. One who rarely left his home state unless it involved Ohio State University football.

Quit complaining. So it's small. Good things come in small packages. Ferraris are small. So are little blue Tiffany boxes. It's even red, your favorite color. How bad could it be?

You'll be riding a scooter in midair—and red just makes it easier for the rescue people to find the debris. That bad enough for you?

Alex shoved the mental argument as far away as possible and focused on the here and now. She could do this. *Had* to do this. After all, she was a professional and professionals didn't balk when met with a challenge.

Besides, David would be thoroughly ticked if he'd sent one of his reviewers halfway around the world only to have them protest a plane ride this close to the end.

But you know, considering your vacation plans have been canceled, there's only one way this day could get worse.

Alex winced. She wasn't going to *think* about crashing.

The important thing was to not let her feelings of guilt over missing Thanksgiving with her family get to her.

And how are you going to avoid the lectures come Christmas?

She was an adult. She had every right to *skip* Thanksgiving in Tennessee if she chose to do so. In the meantime, she'd just thank God she would be out of cell range so she wouldn't have to listen to her family's calls of complaint that she wasn't there when the turkey was carved.

Since your plans were canceled you could go home after the week's up and avoid the sermons.

No. Uh-uh, no way. She wasn't going to do that. Her canceled plans and pitifully small means of transportation to Deadwood Mountain were *not* some sort of cosmic curse. She'd get there, stay for a week, write a review and spend her two weeks' vacation touring Alaska as intended.

It's an itsy-bitsy, teeny-weeny, red-and-white striped—

A combined panic and frustration-fueled whimper escaped her, echoing off the glass in front of her face.

"Sorry to keep you waiting, folks."

The pilot who'd emerged from the Deadwood Mountain Lodge plane greeted the group with a lift of his gloved hand. He gave them a brief, lopsided smile, and Alex frowned. Why did he strike her as familiar?

The man had a mop of dark hair raked back from his forehead in a messy, I'm-a-guy-and-it's-just-hair kind of style. A short, neatly trimmed beard covered the lower half of his face and held a distinguished hint of gray on his chin beneath his lower lip.

Never fond of beards, Alex had to admit the facial hair didn't detract from the pilot's looks. He was ruggedly handsome and considering the tiny lines that fanned out from his eyes like he did his share of squinting in the sun, she guessed him to be in his late-thirties.

"Hey, Dylan. How have you been?"

The pilot's expression warmed at the greeting called by one of two older gentlemen waiting by the gate.

"Ansel, good to see you again. Walter." He shook hands with both gentlemen, his tone lowering as he said a few words Alex couldn't make out.

Shifting away from the men, the pilot raised his voice again. "Could I have everyone's attention? Thanks. First off, welcome to Alaska. My name's Dylan Bower, and I'm your pilot as well as your fishing and bear viewing guide during your stay at Deadwood Mountain Lodge. I, ah, just noticed we're missing someone. Well, we'll find him shortly, but until he shows let's get down to business. You three," he said to three men standing off to the side, "are going with Sam here." Dylan indicated another man standing in the background near the gate door. "Sam, will fly you to the spike camp, introduce you to the hunting guide who will be with you the three days you're there, then fly you back to the lodge to finish out the week. So, if you'd like to come introduce yourselves to Sam…"

Dressed in camouflage pants and carrying thick coats, the three men stepped forward. Their luggage included rifles in soft black cases.

From the research she'd done in preparation for her article and review, Alex knew hunting was not permitted in the vicinity of the lodges so as not to attract bear or other animals. A spike camp was typically a series of tents or cabin-like structures set up in a specified hunting area forty-five to sixty minutes away from the lodge. Once the kill was made under the license of a trained guide or assistant guide, the hunters would fly back to their lodge and their prize transported for them for processing. Businesses here had the act down to a science. No meat was wasted, and no animal population overly hunted.

Alex waited patiently for the instructions to continue, and prayed for their pilot to say Sam and the hunters would be taking the red plane outside, that there was a nice, *large* plane to transport the remaining guests to the lodge.

While the hunters and Sam talked, Dylan Bower scanned the terminal again, skimming over her position near one of the airport's metal support beams. In an instant his gaze jerked back to her, and the furrow between his eyebrows deepened at whatever thought shot through his head.

Hmm, not a good sign, that. Instead of the friendly smile of welcome he'd used with the older men, Dylan looked at her as though he could instantly tell she was going to be a nervous flier. No pilot liked that confidence killer.

Tell him size matters, that oughta help.

Squirming beneath the intensity of his gaze because it *was* so direct, her heart picked up speed when Dylan extracted himself from the men and moved toward her with a purposeful stride.

Alex straightened from her slouched position and tried to smile even though her stomach was knotted up like a hangman's noose.

She had to do this. With her family in Tennessee having a baby boom and her mother trying to set Alex up with every single guy she knew—or else badgering Alex to agree to date her lovely but boring, couch potato boss—reviewing the lodge was the perfect way to avoid yet another confrontation about why she wasn't married and pregnant since her brothers had recently discovered love or the joys of fatherhood.

Still, Lord help them all if she died before giving her mother grandchildren!

Her pilot's long legs carried him across the coffee-stained carpet at a rapid pace and when Dylan finally stopped in front of her, Alex had to tip her head back quite a bit to maintain eye contact. He was a tall drink of water. Not to mention attractive. Looking at him wasn't a bad way to spend the week. So maybe if she focused on him instead of the size of the plane, she could get through this?

He gave her a slight smile, one she returned with way too much nervous enthusiasm considering she had a rule about getting involved with anyone associated with the business being reviewed.

"You're not what I expected."

CLICK TO READ *A HERO IN HIDING*.

TENNESSEE TULANES SERIES
HER SNOWBOUND HERO
THE REBEL'S SECRET BARGAIN
HIS BABY PROPOSAL
THE DOCTOR'S NANNY
A HERO IN HIDING

Ivy James Books
CONTEMPORARY ROMANCE NOVELS

THE STONE GAP MOUNTAIN SERIES

THAT SOUTHERN SUMMER NIGHT

BLIND MAN'S BLUFF

HER UNWANTED PROTECTOR

REDEMPTION ROAD

THEIR SECRET SNOWBOUND CHRISTMAS

OWEN'S RETURN

THE REDEEMING LOVE SERIES

HER REDEEMING LOVE

HIS REDEEMING LOVE

REDEEMING US

MONTANA SKIES SERIES

HER MONTANA COWBOY

HER COWBOY SHERIFF

PROTECTING THE SHERIFF'S DAUGHTER

COWBOY MEETS HIS MATCH

MONTANA CHRISTMAS

SECOND CHANCE HERO

TENNESSEE TULANES SERIES

HER SNOWBOUND HERO

THE REBEL'S SECRET BARGAIN

HIS BABY PROPOSAL

THE DOCTOR'S NANNY

A HERO IN HIDING

OTHER BOOKS:

The Crash Before Christmas

Return to Eden

Ivy James is the alter-ego of Kay Lyons, who now focuses on sweet/clean and wholesome contemporary romance and romantic suspense. For more information about Ivy's slightly sexier novels (or to find Kay's clean and wholesome versions of them as well as her latest titles), please go to Ivy James Author/Kay Lyons Author. Or, find her at one of the following:

@KayLyonsAuthor (Twitter)

Kay Lyons Author (Facebook)

Author_Kay_Lyons (Instagram)

Kay Lyons, Author (Pinterest)

SIGN UP FOR KAY'S NEWSLETTER AND RECEIVE FREE BOOKS, UPDATES ON NEW RELEASES, CONTESTS, PRE-RELEASE BOOK INFORMATION, EXCLUSIVES AND MORE!

AUTHOR BIO

Ivy James is the alter-ego of Kay Lyons, who now focuses on sweet/clean and wholesome contemporary romance and romantic suspense. For more information about Ivy's slightly sexier novels (or to find Kay's clean and wholesome versions of them as well as more new titles), please go to Ivy James Author/Kay Lyons Author. Or, find her at one of the following:

@KayLyonsAuthor (Twitter)
Kay Lyons Author (Facebook)
Author_Kay_Lyons (Instagram)
Kay Lyons, Author (Pinterest)

CPSIA information can be obtained
at www.ICGtesting.com
Printed in the USA
BVHW041515130422
634234BV00008B/428

9 781946 863621